MW01609081

Erotic Research

It was just a little innocent research...

Romance writer Julia Martin is fine with her life, just the way it is. Her simple apartment, successful career and Thursday-night pizza dates with her too-hot-for-words editor Ross are more than enough for her. At least, that's what she thinks until her cat dies.

Ross Philips has spent years lusting after his shy best friend, but fears his rather strong sexual desires will be too much for Julia. When she falls into a depression over the death of her cat and stops writing, Ross decides she needs a change.

His suggestion? Try a new genre—erotica. And, of course, being such a good friend and editor, he even plans to help her do a little research.

Warning: this title contains the following: explicit sex, spanking, anal sex, bondage, toys, graphic language and all sorts of fun stuff.

Tequila Truth

One's the loneliest number. Two's company. Three's a fantasy come true.

The rules of Tequila Truth are quite simple. Shots are poured, a question asked, and only absolute truth can be the answer. Kylie Halston has been playing the game with her roommates, Colt and Heath, since their freshmen year of college.

On his twenty-fifth birthday, Heath poses a question: "What is your ultimate sex fantasy?" While Colt and Heath's fantasies are too hot for words, it's Kylie's sex dream that hits a little too close to home for all of them. Her wish? For a ménage a trois with two men, complete with bondage and a bit of spanking for good measure.

Colt and Heath are only too willing to make Kylie's fantasies come true and they make a proposal—one no-holds-barred, sexed-up weekend where nothing is off the menu. The only question is, come Monday, will their platonic relationship survive the passion?

Warning: you will need to crank up the air conditioning before reading as this title contains all the following erotic goodies: explicit sex, ménage a trois (m,f,m), anal sex, spanking, bondage, and graphic language.

Learning Curves

Mari Carr

A Samhain Publishing, Ltd. publication.

Samhain Publishing, Ltd.
577 Mulberry Street, Suite 1520
Macon, GA 31201
www.samhainpublishing.com

Learning Curves
Print ISBN: 978-1-60504-411-8
Erotic Research Copyright © 2009 by Mari Carr
Tequila Truth Copyright © 2009 by Mari Carr

Editing by Lindsey McGurk
Cover by Scott Carpenter

This book is a work of fiction. The names, characters, places, and incidents are products of the writer's imagination or have been used fictitiously and are not to be construed as real. Any resemblance to persons, living or dead, actual events, locale or organizations is entirely coincidental.

All Rights Are Reserved. No part of this book may be used or reproduced in any manner whatsoever without written permission, except in the case of brief quotations embodied in critical articles and reviews.

Erotic Research, ISBN 1-59998-894-1
First Samhain Publishing, Ltd. electronic publication: March 2008
Tequila Truth, ISBN 1-60504-218-8
First Samhain Publishing, Ltd. electronic publication: October 2008
First Samhain Publishing, Ltd. print publication: August 2009

Contents

Erotic Research

Dedication

For Andrew

Chapter One

"Me and my big mouth," Julia muttered as she dragged in the third load of wood to stack beside the fireplace. The snow hadn't stopped falling since she'd arrived and, while the cabin was certainly toasty, she didn't relish the thought of being buried alive by snowdrifts for the entire winter. Sure, she was used to being alone, but at least at home in New York City, she had the option of personal contact if she desired it. When the walls of her tiny apartment started to close in on her, she could always hit the market or Starbucks to see other human beings.

Coming to Ross Phillips's rustic escape, this extraordinarily luxurious cabin nestled high in the mountains of West Virginia, to start a new novel—especially at the beginning of January— had not been one of her more brilliant plans. Actually, it was Ross's fault—this reckless venture to the wilderness. He'd goaded her into it like he did most things.

"You're in a rut," Ross had told her. "What you need is a change. A major change."

Unwilling to confess to her totally hot, though thoroughly arrogant, editor that he was right, she let him convince her to escape the city in the dead of winter with relatively little fuss. The fact was she *had* been battling boredom with her chosen path in life, although truth be told, when he made the suggestion for change, she thought he'd merely meant she should take a vacation.

Historical romance novelist by trade, she'd spent the last ten years of her life buried in her small apartment with her beloved cat, Duke, writing about damsels in distress, hunky lords and knights, and glorious adventures. In other words, she'd been living inside her head, creating worlds and men who could never exist in this lifetime.

Two months ago, Duke had gone on to that kitty castle in the sky and Julia's world had fallen apart. Depression set in as she realized her best, and now only, friend was her editor—simply because a cat had died.

She hadn't had a date in nearly three years—which was the last time Ross attempted to set her up. Ten minutes into the evening, Julia knew the blind date would end like all the others. The man would never meet the standards she'd set in her mind for the ideal man. Feigning a migraine, she escaped the disastrous dinner before dessert only to be raked over the coals by Ross the next morning for not giving the man a fair chance.

Even now, she could recall his frustration and anger toward her. She could hear his voice like it was yesterday.

"What the hell is wrong with you?" he had yelled into the phone. "Alex Saunders is a great guy. According to him, you didn't give him the time of day."

"I'm sure he is a perfectly nice man," Julia had answered, feeling guilty for not putting forth more effort. She knew Ross was worried about her spending so much time alone; however she couldn't help but be surprised he thought she would be attracted to Alex. "He's just not my type."

"Oh hell, not that again. Jules, we've talked about this. It's 2005, not 1815," Ross said, exasperation thick in his voice.

"I know what year it is, Ross."

"Do you?" Ross asked. "Do you really?"

"We've had this conversation before."

"That's right, we have. And could it be because you insist on turning yourself into an old maid? Christ, Jules, you're nearly thirty years old. It's time to get out there. Live a little."

"I am perfectly happy with my life the way it is and I am not nearly thirty. I'm only twenty-seven. I like my freedom and I don't need a man. Why can't you trust me when I say that?"

"Because it's not normal, Jules. Living in self-imposed seclusion is not normal. When's the last time you got laid?" Ross asked.

"I don't think that's any of your business. You're my editor, Ross, not my pimp!"

"Jesus, Jules," Ross began.

"And my name is Julia. You know I hate that nickname."

"Jules," Ross said calmly, ignoring her request as usual, "honey, you can't stay locked up in that apartment writing romance novels twenty-four seven. It's not healthy."

"I would think you'd be delighted I'm working so hard. My last four books topped the best-seller list and I've won the True Heart award twice."

"Don't insult me, kiddo. I would hope after all the years we've known each other, you would know I consider you a friend, not a client. And as your friend, I'd prefer it if you wrote less and lived more."

Julia's heart softened as she recalled his words to her that day. Ross was a good friend to her. For the past decade, he'd been her main connection to the outside world, which is why she had foolishly agreed to his idea of a change. Rather than suggesting a relaxing cruise, however, his idea of a major change was actually a new genre.

Erotic romance. According to Ross, the market for these hot books was booming. He'd given her a box full of titles, encouraging her to read them and see what she thought.

For the past month, she'd been immersed in capture, bondage, BDSM and ménage-a-trois stories. She learned about domination, submission and the toys—my God, she didn't know such things existed. Butt plugs, whips, paddles, vibrators, nipple clamps. She didn't have a clue about any of these things and now Ross wanted her to write about them. While she had to admit she was intrigued, she also knew no amount of imagination was going to get her out of this mess. Ross had insisted she write erotica and, while still in a sensual haze from her readings and depressed over Duke's death, she'd foolishly agreed to try.

Granted, she was technically not a virgin, but she couldn't help but wonder if there was a statute of limitations on virginity. How long could you consider yourself experienced without actually having sex? She'd had sex with two, almost three men in her life—her high school beau, her college sweetheart and a nearly disastrous one-night stand. While her high school and college boyfriends had both been very sweet men, the bed play had certainly been nothing to write home about—mainly innocent exploration and vanilla sex.

Her lack of experience seemed to be in direct contrast to Ross's wealth of practice and skill. For all the dates she seemed to lack, Ross Phillips more than made up the difference for both of them. Like Baskin-Robbins, he had a flavor of the month and it was always unique, different and exotic. A steady parade of gorgeous women seemed to make their way through his bedroom—so many in fact, Julia teasingly nicknamed him "Hef", likening him to Hugh Hefner and his Playboy Bunnies.

The sad truth was she hadn't had sex in nearly a decade, except for that near miss almost five years ago which had been an unmitigated disaster and the main reason she'd sworn off men and sex forever. She still couldn't think of that night without blushing regret. She'd gone to a Christmas party at the home of one of her publishers and gotten a little inebriated. Actually, she'd gotten a lot inebriated. She hated social events and was terrible at small talk. She was supposed to hang out with Ross, but...

Ross had shown up with Bridget, his buxom blonde on-again, off-again girlfriend, or—as Julia liked to refer to her—slutfriend. The woman looked as if she'd come from the catwalks of Paris, in a shimmering silver dress cut so low in the back Julia was sure one quick turn and her entire rear end would be exposed. She was dripping with brilliant blue sapphires hanging from her ears, neck and both wrists, no doubt an early Christmas gift from Ross.

Julia rolled her eyes as the saying "a fool and his money are soon parted" drifted through her mind. The woman was a barracuda. Once she sank her teeth into a man, she didn't let go until she'd devoured him and his bank account whole. Julia had tried numerous times to convince Ross that Bridget was shallow and money hungry, but he simply teased her about being jealous and continued his unsavory association with the bitch. All Julia could figure was Bridget must be one hell of a lay because two minutes of listening to her imperious demands would make any sane person run for the hills.

Unfortunately, tonight Julia had been counting on having Ross to hang out with, to ease the awkwardness of being there alone, but apparently Bridget, who supposedly wasn't going to be able to attend because of a photo shoot in L.A., must have managed to swing a late flight back to the city.

Much to her relief, Scott Jenkins, one of the company's new accountants, struck up a conversation and Julia, glad to not have Ross see her standing alone looking like a wallflower, was happy to participate. She and Scott spent the night ensconced on one of the couches in the living room laughing and talking and drinking. For once, she felt desirable, even pretty.

Not that she thought she was ugly. The fact was Julia considered herself to be extremely ordinary. Medium height, medium weight, brown hair, brown eyes—boring, boring, boring. She was nothing like the steady stream of supermodels constantly hanging off Ross's arm. Not that she was jealous, like he thought. Well, not too jealous anyway.

From the way Ross kept looking across the room at her, it was obvious he was as surprised as she was that someone was taking an interest in her. Feeling slightly annoyed by that, and more than a little tipsy, Julia continued to giggle and flirt, pleased to be able to rub Scott's interest in Ross's smug face. Maybe now he would finally see her as a real woman, not the little-sister type, whom he constantly felt compelled to take care of and lecture to about her shyness, wasted youth and lack of social life.

Shaking herself for her somewhat-continuing obsession with her editor, Julia tried to focus on the man in front of her. While Scott was attractive, she didn't feel overwhelmed by his appearance as she did with Ross. Ross Phillips was a natural athlete, who towered over her by at least six inches. It was his chiseled face that served as the model for nearly all of her romantic heroes, although she would never tell the cocky bastard that. He already had an overinflated opinion of himself and she considered it her calling in life to be the one woman to help him keep his feet firmly planted on the ground by not gushing over his every word and smoldering look. Not, of course, that he ever directed any smoldering looks toward her.

Glancing across the room, she studied him. He wore his jet black hair longer than he had when they'd first met, and she liked it. In fact, it was this new rugged look of his that had inspired her to write her first pirate novel, which was turning out to be her best-selling book to date. Shaking herself, Julia stifled a groan at allowing her imagination to continue to dream such an impossible dream. Ross Phillips was her publisher and her best friend. That was it. They had a standing Thursday pizza night because in the world of powerful, wealthy, handsome men like Ross, she was not weekend-date material.

Several hours and glasses of champagne later, Julia found herself in Scott's arms as he finally worked up the courage to kiss her. She knew she should be embarrassed by this public display of affection, but her head was fuzzy from the alcohol. His kisses were very nice, soft and warm and she was actually anxious for them to continue. It had been ages since someone had kissed her. Scott must have sensed her acquiescence because he helped her stand, and led her up the stairs to one of the house's beautifully appointed bedrooms.

The rest of the night seemed hazy and slightly unreal as Scott lay across the big four-poster bed with her. She'd missed making out and Scott was certainly reawakening parts of her that had lain dormant for far too long. His lips traveled along her cheek and down the side of her neck. Alarmed, Julia was slightly embarassed to discover her blouse was unbuttoned. It seemed somewhere along the line Scott had grown a few extra hands and she struggled to keep up with them. He was touching her everywhere and yet, when she closed her eyes, it was Ross she saw touching her, kissing her, making her feel so hot. A light breeze touched her thighs as she felt her skirt slowly being lifted and she opened her drowsy eyes, somewhat surprised to find Scott—not Ross—shirtless and digging through his wallet.

"I have a condom in here somewhere," he said. His words hit her like cold water in the face. Guilt suffused her. She'd been fantasizing about Ross the whole time Scott was touching her. He was a very nice man, but she was not the type to succumb to one-night stands. He deserved her whole attention and desire. Unfortunately, she could provide neither.

Reaching down, she attempted to adjust her skirt. "Uh, Scott," she began, "I think maybe we should slow down."

"Don't worry, baby," Scott crooned, "we've got all night. I'm gonna love you good and slow."

His corny line disgusted her. As did her uncharacteristic actions—she didn't have sex with strangers at parties. Attempting to rise, she continued, "No, I don't think you understand. I want to go back downstairs."

"What? Why?" Scott asked, his voice aghast.

"Please, don't get me wrong. I think you are a very nice man, but I don't think we know each other well enough to sleep together."

Scott laughed coldly. "Everybody at the office said you were an uptight bitch, an ice queen. Guess they were right. Well, sweetheart, fact is you should know better than to go to a bedroom with a stranger. Maybe I should teach you a lesson about what happens to a little girl who acts like a cock tease."

"Excuse me?" Julia's voice shook with anger. "Get away from me," she demanded, trying to shake off his viselike grip on her arm.

"No." Scott's voice was infuriatingly calm. "But please feel free to struggle. I like a girl with spirit."

"You—*you*," she stammered, unable for once in her life to come up with the perfect word, the perfect line.

Scott merely laughed as he pushed her back on the bed,

straddling her kicking legs. For the first time since she entered the bedroom, Julia felt the cold, clammy hands of fear seize her. Scott's strength was far superior to hers. He'd seemed like such an affable guy, easygoing and kind. God—what a fool she was.

"I said *let me go*," she repeated, beating on Scott's chest, pushing as hard as possible. Scott continued to laugh until she managed to land one hard slap across his face.

"You little whore," he snarled, returning her slap with an even harder one across her cheek. Bright lights flashed before her eyes as Julia suddenly understood what it meant to see stars. The sound of fabric tearing roused her from the lingering pain and she fought even harder.

"Stop! No," she yelled. Surely Ross or someone from the party would hear her if she screamed, and come to investigate. How embarassing. However, her stomach roiled at the thought of this man touching her in any intimate way. Mortified or not, she needed help.

Before she could make a sound, a familiar, beloved voice came from the doorway. "I believe the lady said no."

Julia had never heard Ross's voice sound so quiet or menacing. Scott immediately jumped off her and the bed, turning to face his boss.

"I think you misunderstand, Mr. Phillips," Scott began. "We were just playing. She likes it rough, pretends to struggle, you know how it is."

"Is that true, Julia?" Ross asked, looking at her for the first time since entering the room. She felt herself blushing as she attempted to cover herself with the remains of her shredded blouse, pulling down her skirt at the same time. Both acts were futile—her hands had chosen that exact moment to begin shaking uncontrollably.

"Good God, no, Ross," she gasped. "He's a pig."

No sooner had the words passed her lips before Ross crossed the room and punched Scott harder than Julia ever imagined a man could. Scott's eyes rolled up into his head as he fell like a sack of potatoes.

"K.O.," she whispered, spellbound by Scott's still form on the floor.

Ross stepped over the unconscious accountant before kneeling at Julia's feet.

"Are you okay?" he asked, his voice so kind and full of concern that Julia felt the dam give way as she fell into his embrace, the shock of the moment evaporating, replaced by delayed terror.

"Oh God," she sobbed as Ross rocked her gently in his arms, whispering soothing words. Her tears flowed, her teeth chattered and her shaking seemed to go on forever. After several long minutes, she struggled to catch her breath before speaking.

"How did you know I was in trouble?" she whispered.

"I'd heard some unsavory rumors about Jenkins around the office. I've been keeping an eye on the two of you all night. Unfortunately, I was detained for a few minutes and when I got back, you and Jenkins had vanished. Did he force you here?" he asked softly. His face was flushed and his own hands were not steady as he reached for the bedquilt and tightened it around her shoulders, studying her face intently.

At her embarrassed blush, she sensed the anger in him begin to rise again as he noticed the red hand print across her left cheek. Taking her chin in his fingers, he turned her face to look at it more closely. The menace she felt building in him seemed almost tangible as he glanced back down at Scott, still prostrate on the floor.

Before he could inflict further pain on the asshole

accountant, she muttered, "No, he didn't force me. I—I mean, he— God, I came here on my own." *Dear Lord.* She'd almost willingly let Scott have sex with her.

"I'm taking you home," Ross said stiffly as he rose and began setting her clothing to rights. Shame suffused her body— Ross was obviously disgusted by her and her actions.

"I'm sorry," she whispered.

"What?" Ross knelt beside her again, pulling her blouse closed and securing it as much as possible, despite the fact several buttons were missing. "What do you have to be sorry for?"

Julia's humiliation came back tenfold as Ross efficiently re-dressed her, gently holding her ankles as he slipped her heels back on her feet. Feeling like a child, she added, "I'm an idiot. I thought he was a nice guy. You must think I'm the biggest fool in the world."

"Oh, Jules, of course I don't think you're a fool. I think you're a sweet, trusting woman who had a little too much to drink. Perhaps you were a bit naïve, but you've never been a fool. The fool was me for leaving you unprotected. I knew what kind of man Jenkins was. I should have yanked you away from him the second I saw the two of you talking. I just didn't think he'd try anything at a work function."

Julia looked at Ross and trembled at the anger she saw lurking in his eyes.

"Ross—"

"Hush, no more words. You look wiped out, Brown Eyes. I'm taking you home."

Julia smiled at this new endearment before realizing she truly was exhausted. Her eyes began to drift closed before another thought opened them again.

"What about Bridget?"

"She's a big girl. She can find her own way home."

"She'll be pissed off," Julia muttered, again fighting back sleep.

"That seems to be one of her two permanent states," Ross answered, gently lifting her into his arms and carrying her across the room as if she weighed no more than a mere babe.

"What's the other state?" she asked groggily.

"Horny. Go to sleep, Jules. I'll take care of everything."

Throwing the last load of firewood on the pile, Julia dropped into the comfy chair in front of the roaring fire, the heat from the flames not the only thing causing her face to flush. She tried not to think of that night, but every now and then it came creeping back to her. She never saw Scott again, although she'd heard through the grapevine Ross had transferred him to God knew where. Asking Ross was a definite impossibility, as they seemed to have reached a tacit agreement never to speak of that night again and she, for one, was glad to avoid the topic. Discussing the biggest act of stupidity of her life with the man of her dreams was something she would never voluntarily do.

All she remembered after falling asleep in his arms that night was waking up the next morning alone in her bed, then managing to avoid him for almost a week before he stopped by with pizza and beer for their standing Thursday-night dinner. He carried in a large pepperoni and mushroom, cracked open a cold one and started talking about his week as if nothing out of the ordinary had happened at the Christmas party. Relieved by the reprieve, Julia followed his lead and avoided the subject.

Staring into the flames, she felt herself slipping back into the same melancholy that had taken over in the past few months. Her life was in the gutter and she had no one to blame but herself. Her parents had been killed in a car crash her junior year in college. Blinded by the loss, she'd cut herself off from everyone close to her. She'd moved out of the apartment she shared with two friends, broken off her relationship with her boyfriend and buried herself in her schoolwork. After graduation, she'd rented a small apartment with the little bit of money left to her by her parents, adopted Duke from an animal shelter and poured herself into her writing. By escaping into her romance novels she was able to exist in an exciting world with dashing men who loved their women no matter what. And in the process, she was able to avoid feeling anything real. If you never truly loved, she reasoned, you never truly lost. Love in a fantasy world was safe and painless. None of her characters ever disappointed her by dying or leaving her.

Unfortunately, she was halfway through writing the third book when she realized her money had run out. Unwilling to leave her emotionless sanctuary, she mailed out her first manuscript to twenty different publishers. Nineteen rejections immediately returned. Then her phone rang. Ross Phillips, a young editor with a struggling publishing company he was launching with a friend, invited her in for a meeting. He saw something special in her writing and thought she had what it took to make it big. The rest, as they said, was history. Her books were an immediate success and they helped to skyrocket Ross's small company into a major contender in the publishing world. Ross was now the chief editor and controlling partner in the firm.

Shaking her head, she chastised herself for falling into the same black despair that had continued to hound her since Duke died. "I'm here to write," she said aloud, desperate to hear a voice in the quiet of the cabin. At least when Duke had been around she'd never felt crazy for talking to herself. She could justify it by claiming she was talking to the cat.

A loud knock at the door had her jumping up. Suddenly feeling very isolated and unprotected, she scanned the room for some sort of weapon. Spying a big log in her pile of firewood, she grabbed it, cowering in the corner. The pounding on the door continued, louder this time, and Julia's heart began to race. Who the hell would be on top of a mountain in the middle of nowhere on a day like this? It was a virtual whiteout outside.

"Jules, open the damn door. I'm freezing my ass off out here."

Ross? She sighed in relief, rushing to unlock the door, and there in the doorway stood her very tall, very wet editor.

"What are you doing here?" she asked, aware her tone was distinctly unfriendly, but he had scared her half to death.

Eyes narrowed, Ross entered the cabin, his arms laden with packages, a large duffel bag thrown over one shoulder, a backpack over the other. "I tried to call, but the phone lines are down," he answered gruffly.

"My cell?" she asked sarcastically.

"No service up here," he replied with equal irritation.

"Is something wrong?" She couldn't imagine what could be so bad it would compel Ross to leave the comfort of his penthouse apartment in New York City to drive for nine hours to the mountains.

"Blizzard." He unloaded his bags on the kitchen counter. "Headed this way. I was worried you'd be snowed in without enough food."

Secretly pleased at his incredibly sweet gesture, Julia smiled and helped him unload the soggy paper bags. "You've brought enough food for an army." She gaped at all the meat, vegetables, fruit and snacks he carried in. "I hope you don't think I need all this to survive. Hey, I didn't hear a car. How did you get here?"

"By the grace of God and my four-wheel drive. I almost made it all the way to the cabin. The snow is already pretty deep. I got stuck about a mile down the road. Had to walk the rest of the way. Looks like we're going to be stuck here for a while." Pulling off his drenched coat, he hung it on the peg by the door.

"My God," she exclaimed, glancing out the frosted window, "it's freezing out there and the visibility must be zero. You're lucky to have made it at all. What the hell were you thinking? You could have been killed." She put her hands on her hips, suddenly aware of the very real danger he'd just escaped.

"What was I thinking?"

"Yes. Good Lord, Ross, of all the idiotic things to do. What if you'd crashed the car? What if you'd gotten lost in the snow while looking for the cabin? You could have frozen to death."

Ross shook his head. Clearly, of all the receptions he'd imagined, this nagging scold was not one he'd considered. "I guess, like the idiotic fool I am, I thought you'd be glad to see me. That you'd offer me a warm drink and some supper. I thought you'd be happy not to be stuck up here in this godforsaken cabin alone in a blizzard!"

Biting her lip, she said softly, "Well, I am. Happy, that is. I was feeling rather trapped—and alone."

As quickly as his anger came, it left him. Smiling, he admitted, "It was a damn stupid thing to do. Unfortunately that fact didn't occur to me until I was about halfway up the mountain and I realized it was too late to turn around."

"Let's get you out of those wet clothes," she said, suddenly very pleased to have him with her. "I'll put some water on for tea."

"Don't bother with the tea. I brought a bottle of Southern Comfort." His hands shaking, he attempted, with little success, to tackle the buttons on his soggy flannel shirt. "We are in the South, after all."

"I'm not sure West Virginia classifies as the South. It's really sort of the middle. Here, let me." Pulling his trembling hands away, she quickly unbuttoned his shirt and tugged it off. His skin was like ice to the touch. "You'll be lucky if you don't catch pneumonia or frostbite," she said, unable to resist one more scold. "Come stand by the fire." Taking his icy hands in hers, she rubbed them lightly. "I'll get a blanket for you. Stay here and try to get warm."

Crossing the room, she retrieved a fleece blanket from the foot of the bed as Ross struggled with the button fly on his damp jeans.

"I'll do that," she said, concerned for his health. His hands were still trembling and looked blood red and chapped. No doubt he'd lied about how long he'd really been roaming around in the snow and wind.

"Jules," he started to object, but she was already working the buttons free, concern distracting her from exactly what she was offering to do. When she had the last button unclasped, she grabbed the waistband and started to pull the clinging denim off his legs. The task was harder than she would have thought, but sheer determination and worry kept her going. She struggled for several minutes, working the material down his muscular legs, stopping only to pull off his boots and socks, before finally peeling the jeans completely off.

"There," she exclaimed, looking up into Ross's suddenly pained face. Her mouth went dry as she realized that during her exertions she'd knelt in front of him and was now eye level with his barely clad cock straining through the material of his silk boxer shorts. This part of him certainly gave new meaning to the term "frozen stiff".

"I—" she stumbled, unwilling to take her eyes off his very large appendage. She was sure she'd never seen anything quite so big and her curiosity outweighed her embarrassment.

"My God," she whispered, awestruck as the monstrous cock seemed to grow even larger before her eyes. Without a thought, she reached up and nearly touched it before a growl above her and a strong hand on her wrist stopped her.

"Brown Eyes," Ross said, his deep voice flowing over her like honey, "if you don't move away from that this minute, I'll keep you kneeling there the rest of the night."

Gasping, Julia rose quickly, painfully aware she was not as averse to his threat as she should be. She'd never sucked on a man's cock before, had never even wanted to until she'd read those damned erotic novels Ross had given her. Now all she could think about was trying to give him a blowjob. Lord, she was losing her mind.

"I'll get you something to eat," she muttered, escaping to the far side of the cabin.

Chapter Two

Ross watched his brown-eyed angel flutter across the room to the kitchen, obviously hoping to escape. The main reason he loved this cabin was because it was a whole house contained in one large room. The roomy kitchen was separated from the rest of the room by a long bar and it contained everything needed to make someone's stay special. An extra-large refrigerator, microwave, convection oven and dishwasher made sure visitors wouldn't starve or slave.

On the opposite wall of the cabin was the tall king-sized oak bed, with a matching dresser, chest and wardrobe. In the center of the room was the large living area, complete with an oversized couch and two easy chairs facing the big stone fireplace, a huge bearskin rug on the floor in front and a double-sided partner desk, one side of which Jules had clearly claimed as her laptop and notes rested there. The only other room in the cabin was the adjoining bathroom with a large Jacuzzi tub and double-headed shower stall. It was a lover's paradise and Ross had known the moment he laid eyes on it he would buy it and bring Jules here. For the first time in their decade-long relationship, his favorite author would have no escape—not from him or his plans for seduction.

He watched as his skittish kitten dropped the fork she was using to flip the ham steaks she'd hastily thrown into a cast-iron skillet. Grinning, he admired her luscious backside as she bent to pick it up. God, she was perfect. Ross shook his head, amazed to think he'd been blind to her beauty for so many years. He and Jules had rocketed to the top of their respective fields together. They had climbed the ladder of success together and foolishly, Ross had wasted the first few years of their relationship treating her like a little sister. Studying her now, he was feeling anything but brotherly.

His feelings for her hadn't changed overnight, but rather evolved gradually after the unsavory incident between Jules and Scott Jenkins. Watching Julia flirt and make eyes at another man had nearly driven him out of his mind that night. He'd never seen her show any interest in another man and the image of her showering all her lovely smiles and lilting laughter on someone else was more than he could stand. Jealousy, in regard to Jules, was a new emotion for him and it took him by surprise.

Of course, it didn't help that she was wearing a sheer red blouse and black velvet skirt shorter than he'd ever seen her don. He was used to seeing her in her tomboy outfits—jeans and T-shirts. Yet that night, she'd obviously taken special pains with her appearance—even wearing makeup and pulling her lovely brown hair up in a chignon, allowing a few wisps to frame her face. Ross's fingers itched during the whole party to yank her upstairs, take her hair down, pull his hands through it and watch it trail over her shoulders.

When he saw her fighting Scott on the bed, her eyes wide with fear, he was overwhelmed with an anger more intense than any he'd ever felt before. For the first time in his life, he knew what it felt like to want to physically hurt another person. Hell, to kill another person. He would gladly have ripped Scott Jenkins to pieces for touching Julia against her will. Later, when he realized she'd willingly gone to the bedroom with Scott, he felt eaten alive with jealousy. The only man he wanted in her bed was him. Somewhere along the line his little Julia had blossomed into a true beauty. Her wavy chestnut hair framed a heart-shaped face and emphasized her large whiskey-colored eyes. Her body was every man's wet dream with firm, large breasts, a narrow waist and shapely hips a man could grab onto as he plunged into her.

Despite the unexpected revelations of that night, he continued to fight his growing attraction to his sexy romance writer, dismissing it as a passing fancy, a strange quirk of fate. For all intents and purposes, she was an innocent and his sexual desires needed an experienced woman, one who could handle his darker appetites. Jules did not fit that bill. Unfortunately, the women who could handle him in the bedroom, women like Bridget, were complete bitches out of bed. For the last few years he'd managed to convince himself he preferred his eligible-bachelor status, hopping from one casual, sex-only relationship to another, while getting the female companionship he craved from his best friend, Jules.

Every now and then guilt would get the better of him and he'd convince himself he was being selfish with Julia, trying to keep her in a little box—his own exclusive friend, his own private fantasy. He knew she would make a hell of a wife for some lucky bastard, even if it couldn't be him. He tried more than once to set her up with other guys, but at the last minute, he'd panicked and found the worst possible man for her. After forcing her to endure several mismatches, he didn't have the stomach to try any more blind dates for fear one of his setups might actually take. Unwilling to risk losing her, he stopped trying to convince her to join the real world. Keeping her busy with deadlines and their Thursday-night pizza dates, he allowed her to convince him she was happy with her life as it was, which in turn, allowed him to hop from bed to bed attempting to satisfy his heavy-handed sexual urges. Then the damned cat died and he watched his best friend fall apart.

For the first time since he met her, Jules stopped writing and Ross realized something else. He was in love with Julia Martin. This quirky, intelligent, shy, inquisitive little romance writer had stolen his heart. When he stopped to think about it, she'd stolen it ten years ago when she'd walked into his dingy little office and struck a book deal with the tenacity of a pit bull. Shy she might be, but stupid she was not. Over the years, they'd fought long and hard over the development of her craft and he had to admit that of all the writers he edited and published, Julia's work was by far the best.

No longer willing to deny his true feelings for her, he was about to put into action the game plan he'd designed a couple of months ago. He was going to claim Jules as his own and all he had to do was open her up to her sensuality, her passion. The erotica suggestion had been the first test. Ross had suggested she try to write a new genre, then gave her books to expose her to all the types of things he wanted to try with her. One evening, four weeks earlier, had set in motion the chain of events leading to this moment. He could still recall every word of their conversation that night.

It nearly killed him to wait until their Thursday-night date to see what she thought of the books he'd given her to read. When he arrived, her face was flushed and she seemed to be having trouble breathing. Glancing at the end table, he saw a copy of one of his favorite BDSM books, *Master Lover*, lying there.

Gesturing to the book, he cleared his throat before asking, "So, what do you think?"

His Jules was nothing if not painfully honest. "It's

amazing," she replied. "Do you think there are people who really live like that?"

Ross nearly came in his pants at her forthright question. "Yeah, I'm sure there are." He shifted slightly before sitting on the couch, adjusting the jeans which had suddenly become too tight.

"Would you live like that?"

Ross choked on the beer he was drinking.

"Sorry," she said, grinning sheepishly. "That was an unbelievably personal question. Don't answer."

Unsure what to say, Ross grabbed a piece of pizza, using the time to stall and think of a way to respond, a way to keep the conversation going, without giving himself away.

"I don't think I would like living like that," she added between bites and Ross's heart fell to his shoes. The test was over and he had failed. He wanted to be with Jules more than anything, but any relationship between them was doomed. There was no way he'd be able to hide the darker side of his sexual nature. Eventually, he would want her tied helpless on the bed. He would want to spank her, control her, fuck every part of her body—her ass, her mouth, her pussy—and according to her, she would balk, reject the idea.

"I mean," she expounded, unaware of his sudden desolation, "it might be fun to try in bed, but I don't think I could subscribe to the lifestyle. I'm too set in my ways and there is no way I could let some guy order me around all day, telling me how to dress, where to go, stuff like that."

The hallelujah chorus began playing loudly in Ross's head. She was willing. He didn't want the lifestyle either. His Jules was intelligent and independent and he loved her that way. The green light to proceed flashed. All systems go.

"Dinner's ready," Julia announced, dragging Ross's thoughts back to the present. So far his plan had gone like clockwork. She had agreed to try her hand at writing the erotica book and when he suggested she come here to write in solitude, she didn't blink twice. He'd intended to give her a few days to struggle over starting the book before stopping by to see how she was doing, but the blizzard sped things up. And not necessarily for the worse. Now he and Jules would be snowed in for days with no chance of escape. All he had to do was convince her that, in the interest of research, perhaps the two of them should try some of the things she was going to write about. His backpack was filled to the brim with sex toys and he intended to introduce her to every one of them.

The meal passed in quiet conversation, the two of them comfortable dinner companions after so many years of friendship.

"How many dinners do you think we've eaten together?" she asked casually.

Ross chuckled. "I don't know. Three, four hundred? And amazingly enough, your cooking never gets any better." He stabbed another bite of charred ham, waving it in front of her face.

"Ha ha," Julia answered. "You would think after so many dinners, you'd wise up and stop asking me to cook."

"Why do you think I designated Thursdays as pizza night?" Ross asked smugly, then deftly dodged the piece of flying ham she flung at him in response.

He rose and grabbed her hand. "Come on. Let's go sit by the fire."

Before dinner, he'd thrown on a pair of gray sweatpants and a faded navy blue T-shirt. Julia admired the way the pants hung low on his hips, yet she couldn't erase the image of him earlier—shirtless as she knelt in front of his enormous erection. She'd never seen him in anything other than his jeans and a T-shirt on Thursdays, or the Hugo Boss designer suits he wore to the office. Seeing his muscular, bare chest with honest-to-God washboard abs still had her libido doing somersaults. How they were going to coexist in this cabin for who knew how long was beyond her. She hoped for her sake he would keep his clothes on and limit his dressing to the bathroom, lest she make a fool of herself by drooling. She was also fairly certain the size of his penis was something she would see in her dreams for the rest of her life. My God. How could any woman accept something that size inside her? Just the thought of it sent shivers down her spine and she felt an unusual dampness seeping between her legs. So much for ignorance is bliss. Julia suspected this new knowledge of Ross's generous bounty was only going to cause her even more sleepless nights fantasizing about something that could never be.

Julia started for one of the soft chairs in front of the fireplace, but Ross intercepted and pulled her down with him to sit on the soft bearskin rug. As night fell, the cabin suddenly seemed very romantic. Attempting to distance herself from the fact she was sitting so closely to her hunky best friend, Julia forced her mind to other subjects. Perhaps a cabin like this could be the setting for her new book. An isolated cottage deep in the mountains during a terrible blizzard. It definitely had potential. Even now, as she and Ross were enveloped in cozy warmth with only the fire to light the room, Julia could easily envision the characters from her erotic novel in just such a place.

"So," Ross said, lying on his side with his head propped on his elbow. Even in such an unassuming pose, Julia couldn't help but feel overwhelmed by his presence beside her.

"How's the book coming?" he asked, as if reading her mind.

"I've only been here a day, Ross. I've barely had time to unpack, let alone start writing."

"Even so," he continued, "I know you, Jules. You've probably been obsessing over the plotline for days. What's it going to be about?"

Julia blushed as she considered his words. Truth be told, she had been imagining the story every night in bed since she'd read the erotica books he'd loaned her—with him cast in the role of the leading man and her as the heroine. She'd even gone so far as to order a vibrator online, although she hadn't worked up the nerve to actually use it yet.

"Well?" he persisted.

"Ross, you know I hate it when you pressure me about a story line. Truthfully, I haven't decided what to write about yet. I'm tossing around a couple of angles."

"Really," Ross said, not the least bit put off. "What angles? Maybe I can help you decide."

"Well," she began, startled by his persistence. Ross never pushed for story lines. He always trusted her to script a plot completely before she asked him to help her tweak it. "I...was thinking about trying one of those...you know." She waved her hand in midair, too mortified to tell him where her fantasy world had taken her.

"No," he said, imitating her vague hand gesture with a grin, "I don't know."

Biting her lower lip, Julia scowled at him. "Ross," she began to protest.

"Domination?" he asked. "Or maybe a kidnapping story where the woman is sold as a sex slave into a harem?"

Afraid Ross might discover how close to the truth he was coming, Julia turned her head to hide the damned blush burning her cheeks. In her fantasy, she was his sex slave. She belonged totally to him, doing anything and everything he asked of her. Thanks to the erotica books he'd loaned her, she now had a wide array of sexual fantasies about him, far beyond the usual missionary-position one she'd indulged in for years. Her favorite one involved him tying her up and forcing her to have multiple orgasms. A purely ridiculous fantasy considering the fact she'd never had a single orgasm and didn't know the first thing about how to have one, let alone several.

"Hmm." He took her chin in his fingers and drew her face back to his. "What are you plotting in that delicious little mind of yours, Brown Eyes?"

"I— I—" she stuttered again. "Domination." She blurted out the word quickly, hoping perhaps he wouldn't hear or understand what she'd said.

"Domination. And what do you know about domination?" He sat up and slowly moved closer to her.

"Only what I've read," she whispered, her gaze dropping to his lips as he moved even closer.

"Jules." His breath was hot against her cheek. "I'm going to kiss you."

"You are?" she asked breathlessly, her tongue sliding along her lower lip.

"Mm-hmm," he murmured, his lips pressed softly against hers, "and then I'm going to help you do a little research for your novel."

With those words, his lips opened against hers and his initial soft butterfly kiss took on a life of its own. His lips bruised hers in his intense efforts to possess her mouth. Julia had never been kissed with such reckless passion. All of her previous lovers had been almost timid in the way they approached her. As if they were afraid she would break. Ross seemed to suffer from no such fear. He used his kiss and his body to push her to her back on the soft rug, coming over her, covering her completely and leaving her feeling helpless and desired all at the same time. Julia could feel his enormous erection pressing against her hot center through her soft lounge pants as he pulled her legs apart and settled between them. Overwhelmed, she tried to draw away, if only to catch her breath, but Ross's large hands captured her head, holding her still for his assault.

"Don't fight me," he said gruffly as he continued to use his tongue, lips and teeth on her mouth. "Don't fight this."

Domination. The word flitted through her mind as his words came back to her. *He's going to help me research. Research domination.*

Her heart began to pound as she feared she understood what he meant by his words. Ross was going to dominate her—sexually. Her too-hot-for-words, untouchable editor was going to teach her about submission. She closed her eyes. "This can't be happening. This can't be happening."

"Why can't it?" came Ross's deep voice above her, rough with desire.

Had she said that aloud? Opening her eyes, one look at his angry eyes told her she had.

"Why can't this happen?" he repeated shortly.

"You can't possibly want me. I mean, you can't want to have sex with me." She was mortified at being so thoroughly trapped under him. Surely he could feel the shape of her body. Surely he realized the gods had not been generous with her—or actually, they'd been a little too generous. She was too short, too chubby and too curvy. Nothing like his usual super-thin, supermodel types.

"Oh, Jules, I definitely want to have sex with you," he

35

answered, slowly grinding his erection between her legs again. "I would think that would be obvious to you by now."

"No, you can't." She struggled to escape his hold, "I mean, look at me, Ross."

Confused, he pushed up on his elbows. "I am, Jules."

"No, really look at me. All of me. I'm not your type, Ross. I'm not even close to your type."

"My type?"

"Bridget, Mallory, Susan, Trudy, Alexis, you know," she said huffily. "The Miss America brigade."

"Jesus, Jules. What have you been doing all these years, keeping records?"

"Get off me," she said. "I refuse to lie here while you make fun of me. Let's face it, Ross. The only reason you're climbing all over me now is because I'm here and we're obviously going to be stuck in this cabin for the unforeseeable future. I refuse to be a consolation prize or a way to pass the time. Now move!"

However, attempting to move Ross was an act of futility. Julia glanced at his face. She would have been wiser to save her hostile words until she was free. Now she was trapped under all two hundred furious, muscular pounds of him.

"Consolation prize?" he bellowed and she winced. "Is that what the hell you think? That I want you because you're the only woman here? That's quite an opinion you have of me, Jules. I'm surprised you can stomach being in the same room with such an undiscriminating womanizer. The past ten years in my presence must have been pure hell for you."

"Ross," she began, hoping to calm him down enough to encourage him to get off her.

"God damn it, woman. Don't you have eyes in your head? Are you so dense about men that you can't tell when a man desires you? I get a fucking hard-on every time we're in the same room together. You want to count how many dinners we've eaten together? While we're at it, why don't we count how many nights I've spent whacking off thinking about you and your pretty face?"

Julia stopped struggling, stunned. He wanted her. She made him hard.

"And another thing," he continued, still livid, "how dare you paint me as some shallow asshole who only screws supermodels. I'd take you and your sweet, scrumptious body over twenty Bridgets any day of the week."

Scrumptious body, she thought. *He thinks my body is sweet.* Still amazed, Julia didn't even react when Ross rose, pulling her up with him. Her brain didn't begin to function until he dragged her over to the bed with him, where he promptly sat, pulling her facedown over his lap like a recalcitrant child.

"Wait," she cried. "What are you doing?"

"Research," Ross replied, somewhat calmer than before.

"What kind of research?" she asked, her struggles to rise futile against his strength.

"I thought we'd start with a spanking." His voice returned to its familiar teasing lilt.

"Spanking!" she shrieked. "Stop joking around, Ross."

"I'm not joking, Julia," he said so seriously she stopped moving and looked over her shoulder into his face.

"You aren't?"

"No, Jules." Reaching up, he brushed her hair out of her face. "Nothing I want to do to you will be a joke." With his words, his left hand drifted down her back until she felt him tugging at the waist of her pants.

"Ross, wait." Julia resumed her struggling. "Can't we at

least talk about this?"

"Why, Jules?" he asked earnestly. "Can you really say you don't want this as much as I do?"

Julia stopped moving completely as Ross continued to strip away her pants. She felt them slip past her ankles and heard them hit the floor. Ross's hand returned to her bare bottom and she winced, expecting him to hit her. Instead, he ran his callused hand over her sensitive skin.

"So soft," he muttered. "Spread your legs, Jules." His fingers lightly brushed over her ass.

Julia moaned at the hypnotic feeling of his hands stroking her so tenderly.

"Tell me, Jules. Tell me you want this," he pleaded, but the magic of his hands on her body left her speechless. The fact was, she did want this. She had wanted it for years and now that it was happening, she could only revel in the marvelous feelings he was producing.

Without thought, Julia opened her legs, gasping as he dipped his hand lower toward her wet opening. Mesmerized, she felt reality slipping, giving way to the fantasy she'd dreamed of for nearly a decade.

"Christ," he whispered, dipping his finger into her pussy, "a man could drown down there."

Julia wiggled, trying to dislodge his hand, suddenly embarrassed by his words. "I'm sorry," she said miserably, silently cursing her lack of experience. The fact that he could tell how much his touch, his words, his threats of an erotic spanking turned her on was simply too much. What must he think of her?

His chuckle brought her hackles back up. "Sorry?" he said. "You're heaven on earth, Brown Eyes, and you're sorry for it? It's too late for apologies and it's too late to stop. Now hold still."

With that, he brought his hand down upon her bottom—harder than she expected. Shock coursed through her. The pain of the blow fueled the growing fire inside her. He spanked her five more times, each time his hand hitting a different area and each time the pain increasing the pleasure flowing through her. Soon, she began to anticipate and even look forward to the next strike. He stroked his finger around her swollen bud, pressing lightly at first and then with added pressure, while his other hand caressed her sore bottom.

"Oh my God, Ross," she cried, moving against his hands, trying to get closer to the magic he was performing with his fingers.

"Hush. Let me take care of you, Brown Eyes."

"But, Ross," she said, feeling herself at the brink of something she didn't recognize, her body shaking uncontrollably, "it feels too good. I don't know what to do. I can't take this."

"Of course you can, Jules. You're going to take everything I give you and then you're going to beg me for more." His light touches on her clitoris became stronger, his movements faster.

"No." Julia shuddered, suddenly desperate to escape the sensations he was creating inside her. "Please stop. I told you. I don't know what to do." Tears began to fall down her cheeks and she quickly tried to swipe them away. She couldn't make a fool of herself in front of him.

Ross paused briefly. "What to do? Jules, I'm going to make you come. Haven't you ever had an orgasm before?"

"No," she whispered miserably, trying once again to escape his hold. "I can't. Please let me go." She tried to move, but Ross held her down tightly, still across his lap.

"Angel," he said, "I'm a little confused here. You'll just have to bear with me."

"Confused?" She attempted to relax, despite the fact she felt silly in the position.

"Brown Eyes, you can describe an orgasm to perfection with words. I know—I've read every single one of your books. Now, I find out you've never actually experienced one."

She narrowed her eyes. "I happen to have a marvelous imagination. Besides, I do read and do research, you know."

Ross burst into laughter and Julia's temper erupted as she beat her fists against his thighs—the only part of him she could reach.

"Jules," he said, restraining her with seeming ease, his voice laced with mirth, "I won't tell you again not to fight me."

"Why are you doing this? It's humiliating enough without you laughing at me." His continued torture infuriated her. He'd proven—yet again—that she was an inexperienced, naïve fool. How many more times tonight was he going to make her feel stupid, unsophisticated, unworthy of his attention? She simply couldn't compete with the Bridgets of the world.

"Humiliating?" Slowly, he turned her over and cradled her in his lap. "Oh, Jules, I'm not trying to humiliate you. I just want to show you what you're missing. Look at me," he demanded, lifting her chin to face him. "Look at me, Jules."

Slowly, she raised her eyes to his, almost surprised to see Ross. Her same, sweet, comfortable friend Ross. He smiled at her and she couldn't stop herself from responding in kind.

"I've made a mess of this, haven't I?" he asked. "As far as seductions go, I have to admit, this has been my worst."

Unwilling to hear Ross berate himself, Julia immediately tried to console him. "Oh no. This isn't your fault. It's mine. I— I'm afraid I don't know exactly how to do all of this. It's been a long time since a man has touched me. A very long time, I'm afraid."

"All the more reason why you should let me help you do a little research. Otherwise how will you be able to write your book?"

"I'll never be able to write that damn book, Ross. Look at me. I'm a sex disaster." She tried to cover her bare bottom with her T-shirt somewhat desperately, suddenly embarassed to be so exposed.

"Not a disaster, Jules, just inexperienced. I could help you with that, if you would let me."

"Help me how?" she asked. His earlier promise to help her research her novel still rang in her ears. Ross always had a plan and Julia shuddered to think what his devious, gorgeous mind was plotting.

"I think I've made it fairly obvious that I'm attracted to you. I have been for quite some time. Why don't we work on this project together? I want you—very badly—and you need more experience—sexually. We could explore some of these things together."

"Things?" Julia asked. *What does that mean?*

"Jules, haven't you ever wondered what it would be like between us? We've known each other nearly a third of our lives. In our work and in our friendship, we're completely compatible. Wouldn't you like to see if the same holds true in bed?"

"So this is just an experiment?" Julia was disgusted at the prospect of having mind-blowing sex as if it were some sort of science project. She was about to refuse, but his next words stopped her.

"No," Ross interjected quickly. "Absolutely not. I'd simply like to take our relationship to another level. Come on, Jules. What do you say?"

Chapter Three

"R-relationship?" Julia stuttered and Ross realized he'd made a grievous error. His Julia was terrified of anything even resembling love or a serious relationship.

"Jules, honey," he said, adopting a carefree tone, "I'm horny as hell for you. You've become an itch I'm dying to scratch. Can you honestly tell me you haven't wondered how it would be— between us?" Desperate to end the conversation, Ross slowly let his hands wander back down to her hot pussy, prodding gently at her wet opening.

Julia's eyes went wide and he watched as she struggled to continue their argument. The words died as he turned up the heat by leaning down to press his lips softly to hers. She moaned as his mouth skated over her lips and he continued his assault. Breaking the kiss, he studied her until he was sure all her damned overanalyzing thoughts were swept away by the pressure of his hands on her body.

At a loss as to how to convince his shy angel to take a chance on him without feeling threatened, Ross took the coward's way out. Rather than speaking, he let his hands do the talking. He knew Julia's main problem in forming lasting relationships was her fear of losing someone she loved. Her parents' untimely deaths had wrecked her emotionally. Without any other family or friends around her at the time, she had no anchor to cling to and so she escaped into her own false reality. Hiding behind her writing exacerbated the problem as she allowed the lives and romances of her characters to satisfy her socially. Pretending to be the heroine in her novels, she could flee the dangers a true liaison would involve. In her mind, love equated loss and after so many years alone, she seemed unwilling to take that risk again.

Of course, the cat dying hadn't helped his cause either. The fresh loss of the beloved creature only served to magnify the pain of losing a loved one again. The only way Ross could see himself forming a lasting relationship with her was by tricking her into it. If she thought he was only having sex with her to scratch an itch and help her with her new book, she would be more willing to take the chance. And once he had her addicted to his touch and attention, it would be only a small step to getting her exactly where he wanted her—in his bed, home and life. Permanently. At least that was what he hoped.

When he felt her reaching the peak once again, he asked, "Haven't you ever dreamed about this? About us?"

"You'll laugh at me if I tell you about my dreams," she replied breathlessly.

"Am I in them?" he teased.

Her sudden blush answered his question.

"Ah ha. Why the hell would I laugh at you? For fantasizing about me? Brown Eyes, that would be a compliment, not a joke."

"Ross, I'm not exactly, you know." She waved her damned hands around again as if that action should explain everything.

"No, I don't know."

"I'm not beautiful," she said quickly, in her too-forthright fashion, unleashing all her fears on him at once. "My boobs are too big, my ass is lumpy, I'm carrying at least twenty pounds too many and I have no idea how to have an orgasm. What on earth could you possibly find desirable about any of that?"

Smiling, Ross bent down to kiss her adorable nose. "Your tits are gorgeous, your ass absolutely grabbable, I hate thin women, and I can teach you how to have an orgasm in about a minute and a half. Any other questions?"

"Is grabbable a word?" Some of her previous tension disappeared as she graced him with a shy smile.

"In regards to your delectable rear end, it should be. I'll put in a call to Webster's as soon as we get back to the city and make sure they include it in the next edition of the dictionary."

"You really want me?" she asked again, clearly unable to believe his words.

"More than anything. Willing to give it a try?" His hands gripped her waist in a manner he was certain betrayed his need.

"Well, I suppose, in the interest of research, I could be persuaded. I have this unbelievably demanding editor who is insisting on an erotic novel."

"Man sounds like a slave driver," Ross joked, thrilled to be teasing a half-naked Jules in bed.

She laughed. "Well, with any luck he is."

Ross's cock rose another three inches. "Talk about tugging on the tiger's tail. Are we finished talking now?"

"Yes, we're finished talking." She snuggled closer to him.

"There's this saying that comes to mind." Ross lifted Julia up and placed her on her back in the center of the bed.

"What saying?" Julia asked breathlessly.

"Start as you intend to finish."

"What does that mean?"

"It means, get ready, Brown Eyes, because I've had ten years to think of all the ways I want to take you and I intend to try every one of them before we leave this cabin."

"Oh my," she answered breathlessly as Ross leaned over to claim her lips again in his possessive kiss.

Nipping lightly on her lower lip, he pushed his tongue into her mouth forcefully, showing her in no uncertain means how he intended to have her. Fast and hard. He paused briefly to lift her T-shirt over her head and watched Julia blush all the way up from her toes. She looked sexy as hell, lying beneath him, totally naked while he was still fully dressed.

"No bra?" he asked, his fingers skimming the tops of her breasts.

"I wasn't expecting company." Her breath caught on the words as Ross bent and took one nipple into his mouth.

"I like knowing you're naked underneath your clothes. Ready for me." He lightly bit the sensitive bud and was pleased by the moan that escaped her lips.

"Oh my God," Julia muttered again as Ross laughed.

"I think I'd prefer 'Oh my master', but whatever works for you," he teased, pulling away to kneel beside her.

Julia blushed once again at his close scrutiny and he watched her lift her arms slightly to cover her body with her hands before apparently changing her mind and lowering them again. He loved all of her many facets—innocence wrapped in a sexy package, shyness mixed with just enough minx, and curiosity overwhelmed by full-blown desire. Her hazel eyes asked questions his body couldn't wait to answer.

Suddenly the intensity of the moment seemed to catch up to her and he watched as she attempted to stifle a giggle.

Grinning, Ross asked, "What's so funny?" as laughter

shook her body.

"I'm sorry," Julia said after a few moments, gasping for breath as her laughter became even more unrestrained. "I can't believe we're actually doing this."

"Why not?" Ross asked, pleased to see her so happy. He loved Julia's sense of fun and having her laughing in his arms, nude in his bed, was probably as close to heaven as he'd ever been.

"It just seems so strange. I mean, it's us."

"Us?"

"You and me, us," she answered as if her explanation made perfect sense. "I mean, I'm lying naked in bed with you. You're my editor, for God's sake. My best friend and self-appointed big brother. We've known each other forever and a day and, I don't know—" she stumbled, struggling to find the right words, "—I suppose I never really thought we'd do something like this."

"Never?" Ross asked suspiciously. He'd caught his shy little writer casting glances at him before when she thought his back was turned. He refused to believe this attraction of his was totally one-sided.

"Well," Julia began, a fresh blush staining her lovely cheeks, "I mean, maybe, I wondered what it would be like."

"Just wondered?" Ross teased. "What about those hot fantasies?"

"Ross." Julia playfully slugged him on the shoulder. "You're my editor. That would hardly be professional."

"Oh, Jules, I can assure you nothing I plan to do to you tonight is going to be professional. It's going to be hot and raw, rough and passionate—and extremely unprofessional."

Squirming at his heated words, Julia reached up to pull him down to her for a kiss, but Ross resisted.

"Not yet, Brown Eyes." Rising from the bed, and without breaking eye contact, he slowly pulled his T-shirt over his head. His erection grew as Julia licked her lips and he couldn't wait to wrap his arms around her, claim her as his own. She glanced down at her own body, then her hand stole out to the blanket at the foot of the bed, no doubt to cover herself.

Sensing her worries, Ross leaned over the bed, drawing his hand down her side, gripping her hip lightly. "You're beautiful," he murmured. Her eyes lit up at his words—and he saw her begin to accept the sincerity of his feelings. "I've never seen a lovelier woman."

Rising again, he quickly shed his sweatpants, revealing the fact he was also lacking undergarments. The erection Julia had studied so intently by the fire, no longer concealed by thin boxer shorts, stood erect from a mass of springy curls.

Worry lines creased her forehead as he bent to kiss her again.

"Don't worry," he whispered against her cheek. "We'll go slowly the first time. I know it's been a long time for you and I won't hurt you."

"Ross," Julia started, her voice thick with desire, but before she could say more, Ross swallowed her words with his own lips upon hers. His hands worshipped her in time with the movement of his mouth, caressing her everywhere. No part of her body was safe from his exploration.

"I want you," he growled, as he took her bottom lip between his teeth. "Open your legs for me, Jules. Show me how much you want me."

Spreading her legs, she gasped as Ross firmly gripped her knees, separating them even farther. Moving his hands up her inner thighs, he circled her swollen bud once more, slowly increasing the pressure. Each time he brought her to the precipice, he'd pull back, leaving her begging for something more, something he knew she couldn't understand or anticipate, something she'd never experienced before. Ross felt his alpha male come to the forefront as he relished the thought of giving her her first orgasm. He intended to make it one she would never forget. Each time he sensed her imminent explosion, he backed off, denying her her release. He continued to torment her until she pounded her fists on his chest.

"Now!" She yelled the word at him and Ross could see in her face she would not be refused again. "Now, damn you!"

In response to her demand, Ross plunged two fingers into her hot cave while his thumb increased the pressure on her clit. The extra stimulation did the trick and Julia fell over the cliff, her joyous scream music to his ears.

Gasping for breath, he watched as she slowly came back to herself on the bed, her gaze drowsy and relaxed when it finally landed on him lying fully beside her, one elbow bent beneath him, holding him up and over her. Never before had he felt such closeness to a woman and he hadn't even found his own release yet. Julia was a gem, a priceless treasure to be cherished and adored.

"That was longer than a minute and a half." Her words were spoken with a breathless chuckle.

"Complaining?" Ross added to her jest. "I could make you suffer even longer next time, Jules. In fact, I plan to."

"No! You nearly killed me."

"Ah," he replied, "but what a way to go."

Reaching up, she bestowed such a gentle, sweet kiss on his lips that Ross felt tears well in his eyes.

"I like being your first," he whispered, his lips making their way down her throat, toward her breasts. "So many firsts," he mumbled, sucking her nipple fully into his mouth. "So many things to teach you." Increasing the pressure of his lips on her, he slowly slid his hand back between her legs.

"Ross," she said breathlessly, "I want you so much."

"Soon, Brown Eyes," he replied. "Very soon."

His fingers found their destination, circling the entrance to her body. Finding her wet heat, he groaned with pleasure against her breast. Sliding two fingers into her, he was aware of the fact that the intensity of his touch was driving her ever closer to yet another orgasm.

"Now," she repeated and Ross grinned to himself. His sweet little innocent was turning into a serious wildcat in bed. He relished her demands and found himself caught up in the heat of the moment as well.

Adding another finger to the first two, Ross concentrated on stretching her. She was tight as a virgin and he knew it was bound to be a bit painful for her in spite of his attempts to ease her. She arched her back as his fingers moved in and out of her with increasing speed. He relished the feeling of her body pushing toward his movements.

"More." She tugged at his wrist, apparently desperate to feel his cock inside her and not just his fingers. "Please, Ross, I need you. Now."

"Dammit, Jules. You're too tight. We have to take this slow."

"No. I can't wait anymore," she cried. "Now. Ross, now!"

"Damn you." Crawling over her, he placed his erection at her opening. He'd entered only a fraction of an inch before freezing.

"Condom," he muttered, amazed at how close he was to entering her without protection. Never had he lost his head so completely. He'd never had sex without a condom in his life.

"Now," she cried. "God, Ross, please. It's okay."

Her answer caught him off guard. There was nothing he wanted so much as to take her right then, skin to skin. However, one of them needed to keep a level head. Indecision kept him still, the head of his cock just inside her, the desire to slam into her so overpowering he felt light-headed. Passion was clearly winning, overriding common sense. Gritting his teeth, he started to pull out, but Julia quickly wrapped her legs around his waist, tight as a vise.

"Jules," he panted, grasping at one last attempt at sanity.

"Now," she whispered, her legs holding him locked in place. "I want to feel you. Only you."

The battle lost, Ross gave in, his craving to feel her without the obstruction of a condom obliterating his own willpower.

In spite of her desperate pleas and the tightening of her thighs about him, Ross reined in his need enough to slow his entrance. Every nerve in his body demanded release and it was all he could do not to pound into her tight, hot body in one hard thrust.

Each inch he penetrated was pure torture—heaven and hell combined. Her strained, panting breaths didn't penetrate his consciousness until he finally filled her completely. Sweat dripped from his brow onto her cheek as he hissed, "Does it hurt?"

"Yes," she cried, through clenched teeth. "Move. I need more."

Ross felt the demons he'd kept at bay until now released full force. With only a short retreat, he returned to fully impale her to the hilt. He stopped at the sound of her screams, worried he'd harmed her before realizing she was coming again with a strength he'd never thought possible. The power of her orgasm drove him over the edge, milking the seed from his cock with an almost-painful grip.

"Jesus," he groaned, amazed by his sudden loss of control. He prided himself on being a man who could ride a woman all night, but his brown-eyed girl had driven him to orgasm with just one thrust. Something that hadn't happened to him since he was a damned teenager. Then another truth hit him like a brick to the head, reality plummeting him to earth. He'd intended to pull out before he came.

"Oh hell, angel," he muttered. "No condom. Jules, please tell me you're on the pill."

When she didn't reply right away, he continued, "I'm so sorry. I've never had unprotected sex before, Jules. I swear it. Christ, I can't believe I didn't use a condom. I'll take care of you, sweetheart. I swear it. No matter what happens I will always take care of you."

"Ross," she said, interrupting his self-deprecation, "it's okay. I'm on the pill."

"You are?"

"Yes," she answered, clearly embarrassed by the conversation. "My, um, periods were pretty painful—cramps and all that. My doctor suggested birth-control pills. She said they would help and, well, they did." Just when Ross thought she couldn't blush any deeper, she proved him wrong. After what they'd just experienced together, he was floored by the fact she could still turn deep red by simply saying the word "period" to him.

"Christ, Brown Eyes, you're killing me."

"I am?" she asked quietly, still unable to meet his eyes.

"Look at me." He tilted her face up to his. "I'm glad you're on the pill, but I still owe you an apology. I'm the more experienced partner here and I put you at risk. I swear to you I'm clean."

"Ross," Julia interrupted, "it's not like I gave you much choice."

"Still, I've never been so careless...or so quick. I haven't come that fast since I was fifteen," he added, shaking his head in disbelief.

Julia laughed. "Must be me," she teased. "I'm so irresistible, you know."

"Is that right? You should have warned me." He tickled her as she giggled uncontrollably. "All right, woman," he said, "it's time to get serious. We have research to do."

"Research," she repeated with mock seriousness. "How could I forget? What did you have in mind?" Her deep brown eyes sparkled in the firelight. With the sheet pulled loosely around her and her long hair in disarray on the pillow, Ross could only stare—stunned speechless, taken aback by her tousled, well-loved look. His best friend had never looked so beautiful or so eager.

"What?" she asked coyly.

"You really are irresistible," he said, the words escaping his lips without a thought.

"I was kidding, Ross." She rolled her eyes, but her genuine smile betrayed her pleasure at his words.

Shaking his head, Ross reached for her, unable to resist her girlish delight at his simple praise. She was obviously starved for appreciation and attention and he fully intended to rectify that oversight, starting tonight. However, his unintentional slips were going to give him away before he was ready to reveal his true feelings. He needed to carefully guard his intentions. Julia needed time. Time for her to become accustomed to having him in her bed as a lover as well as in her life as a friend.

"Up," he ordered, pointing toward the bathroom. "Time for

another first."

"Oh?"

"That is unless you've already been skinny-dipping in a Jacuzzi with an editor with a gigantic hard-on."

Tapping her lips with one finger, Julia looked as if she were trying to recollect such an event. "Hmm." Ticking off the list on her fingers, she asked, "Skinny-dipping, Jacuzzi and horny editor—all of them together, not separate, right?"

"Let me put it this way, Brown Eyes," Ross said, hands on his hips as he glared down at her from the side of the bed. "I find I enjoy being your first in all things, editorially and sexually, so maybe you shouldn't try too hard to remember."

"Oh." Julia giggled. "So I should let you play caveman while I pretend to be a chaste virgin and let you do all sorts of unspeakable things to me?"

"Now you're getting it." Reaching down, he picked her up.

"Ross," she cried, swatting at him, "put me down. You'll hurt yourself."

"Jules," Ross berated, "if you make one more ridiculous comment about your weight, I'll turn you over my knee again. I bench press more than you'll ever weigh at the gym every day."

"But—"

"No buts," he interrupted, carrying her across the room to the bathroom. "Time for a nice hot soak. You must be sore."

"Not really." She squirmed slightly and he sensed she was still uncomfortable with her nudity in his presence. He also suspected she was feeling painful twinges in unfamiliar places. A long, hot bath was just what she needed.

As he set her down, she reached for a towel, only to have him lightly swat her hand away.

"No," he said firmly. "No hiding. Not from me, not here. I

53

like looking at you."

Julia blushed. "I like looking at you too."

At her words, his already-rejuvenating erection rose to nearly full mast. Once the tub was filled, Ross added some soaking salts and turned on the jets before lifting Julia up and over the rim to place her on one of the benches.

"Ah," she breathed, sliding down deeper in the hot water, "this is heavenly."

Joining her, Ross had to agree.

After years of friendship, the two were able to sit in companionable silence without feeling uncomfortable. Ross watched as Julia's peaceful face lost some of its relaxed bliss. Her eyebrows lowered and the crease that often came between them when she was tense or worried made an appearance. *That didn't take long.* He had expected her to begin to question the wisdom of their actions long before now, and forced himself to let her form her questions and concerns. He was ready to set her mind at ease. He'd plotted for weeks about this adventure and he was determined to have his own way. Ross was going to overcome her fear of loss to conquer her heart and claim it as his own. This was the battle of his life and Ross had no intention of surrendering or retreating. Before they left this cabin, it was her white flag he expected to see on the horizon.

Trying to appear relaxed, Ross closed his eyes and leaned his head back against the edge of the tub. He didn't have long to wait.

"What happens when we leave here?" she asked.

Ross opened his eyes, but didn't lift his head. "Here?"

"The cabin."

"What do you want to happen?" he asked, throwing the ball back into her court.

"I—I don't know," she stuttered. No doubt she was shocked he was leaving it up to her. He rarely gave a woman the upper hand in his liasons and Julia knew it.

"I mean, I can't live without you as my editor or my friend," she continued. "If what we're doing here is going to jeopardize that, I want to stop right now."

"Jules, I will always be your friend, I promise you that, but I have every intention of riding this train to the end. There will be no stopping along the way for cold feet."

"Ross, we're both adults. You know as well as I do sex changes things, complicates them. I know the relationships you've had, especially lately, are fairly casual, but even you have to admit, when they ended, everything ended. You don't see any of your ex-girlfriends, period—not as friends, not even as acquaintances. I don't want this to continue if we can't go back to the way things were. I would hate not having you in my life anymore."

"Oh, Jules. What we do here isn't going to affect our friendship. I'm not sure when you started seeing me as such a heartless prick, but you must know after all these years I'd rather cut off my left arm than hurt you. Besides, there is one major difference between you and the other women in my past that you seem to keep forgetting."

"What's that?" Julia asked, attempting to move away from him on the bench.

Ross halted her escape by wrapping his arm around her shoulder and pulling her toward him.

He grinned as he recalled her earlier comments. "What did you call them?" he teased. "Oh yeah, the Miss America brigade. Jules, I was never best friends with any of them. Hell, I was never even friends with them."

"That doesn't seem like something to brag about." Her dry

words were so familiar, Ross laughed.

"Besides, you're forgetting something important."

"What's that?" she asked.

"We've already done the deed, Brown Eyes, and there's no taking it back."

Sighing, she leaned against his arm and he felt some of the tension leave her.

Testing the water, he added, "Are you saying you would want to see this evolve into a real relationship?"

His answer was painfully apparent as Julia blanched.

"R-real relationship?" She glanced away from him. "Don't be silly."

Well, he couldn't blame her for not wanting to rush into a relationship with a confirmed bachelor such as himself. Clearly, he had a lot of work to do to convince Julia he was sincere. While he considered their long-term friendship a blessing, he'd be a fool not to realize it was a detriment as well. Julia knew him better than anyone in the world—his parents included. She knew that nowadays he never stayed with the same woman for more than a month. His last long-term relationship had been with Bridget and that ended over four years ago.

"Relax, Jules," he said quickly. "I know how you feel about relationships. That's not what I'm pushing for." The lie tasted bitter on his tongue and his temper flared briefly at her obvious relief.

"So, we'll just go back to being friends after this," she said without question, as if trying to picture the end of this brief romantic interlude in a few days when the snow began to melt.

Unwilling to risk putting a deadline on the most incredible sex of his life, Ross shook his head. "Sweetheart, the barn door is open and the cow's not coming back. You can't expect to give me only a sample of all the sweetness you have to offer and then not allow me to gorge myself at the feast."

"Good God." Julia laughed. "I have no idea what you just said."

Ross joined in her laughter. "I'm not finished fucking you yet."

Julia winced at his crude comment before asking, "So that's what this is? Fucking?"

Reaching over, Ross pulled her over to him, positioning her legs on either side of his hips until she was straddling him. Placing his erection at her warm opening, he gently prodded before adding enigmatically, "Researching."

With that, he placed his lips over hers, giving her the most incredibly sensuous kiss of his life. With his lips and tongue, he gave her everything he had to give, slowly sliding into her tight, hot pussy until he reached the hilt. With firm hands on her hips, he lightly lifted her up, then pulled her back down, setting a slow, easy pace.

"Ride me, Brown Eyes," he whispered against her moist cheek, the heat of their joining combining with the strong jets of water powerfully enough to create a tidal wave of passion.

Increasing the speed, Julia amazed him again as she took control of the trip, clinging tightly to Ross with her knees on his hips and her arms on his shoulders. Frantic to reach her peak, she set a grueling pace that left Ross desperate to hang on. Julia's passionate nature was constantly astounding him, taking him unaware and leaving him reeling in the wake.

"Ross," she cried, her orgasm fast approaching. Leaning over, she kissed him, nipping his bottom lip, drawing blood, as her climax shook her entire body. "Oh God."

Losing himself in the strength of her powerful convulsions, Ross gave himself up to his second climax in an hour. How had he spent ten years in this woman's presence and failed to notice the tigress raging beneath?

Julia placed her head on his shoulder and Ross felt her slipping into sleep. Tucking her more tightly against him, he lifted her from the water. He reached for a towel, then carried her back to the bed and placed her in the middle to gently dry her off. Exhausted from her exertions, Julia never stirred. Once she was dry, he climbed in beside her, wrapping her up in the soft blanket and his arms.

"Sleep well, Brown Eyes," he whispered as sleep came to claim him as well.

Chapter Four

It was still dark when Julia felt something stir behind her. Startled, she came fully awake, uncertain of her surroundings for a split second. A soft *sshh* wafted by her ear and she recalled everything. Ross, the research, the greatest sex of her life, an orgasm—no, three! All of it came back to her in a rush and she smiled into the dark room—feeling happier than ever before.

Attempting to roll over, she stopped as she realized her hands were tied together above her head and anchored to the headboard. A slight tremor of fear coursed through her body until she remembered she was with Ross, who would never hurt her.

"Ross," she started, only to be silenced by a light smack on her buttocks.

"Hush," he said harshly, his voice strangely different. "You will only speak when asked a direct question."

"What?" she asked, only to be spanked again, this time harder than the first.

Leaning over her, Ross whispered in her ear, "Don't make me gag you. I want you to be able to beg me for everything I'm going to do to you."

A shiver of anticipation flowed through her. With her hands securely tied, Julia had never felt so helpless—or aroused.

Ross began to speak again, his voice farther away as Julia listened to him cross the room. The sound of logs being thrown onto the fire told her where he had gone.

"There's no use screaming," he said, his voice again foreign to her. "Your ship has been sunk, your men killed. You are the sole survivor and your life will only be spared so long as you do as you are told."

A fantasy, Julia thought, considering his words. He'd taken her captive. Excited beyond belief, she remained quiet and still on the bed as Ross continued to draw the picture in her mind.

"My men found you and had every intention of taking you, using you themselves. Imagine how dismayed they were when I claimed you. It's the captain's right, you know, to choose his portion of the spoils first. We've been at sea for nearly six months. So many men desperate for a woman's body. I may still give you to them. If you fail to please me."

Julia whimpered slightly, the fantasy becoming real to her. She was a character in her own book—Ross taking on a role of her own creation. *My Pirate Lover* was one of her latest books and the fact that Ross was taking on the role she'd created with him in mind caused her to go wet with anticipation, wondering what he would do next. She was amazed to discover what a powerful effect his words were having on her. Ross's superior attitude, his tone of voice, his understanding of the character was so authentic she could almost imagine the room was swaying like a ship at sea.

Closer now, Ross leaned over the bed, his hand lightly caressing her bare bottom. She was startled to realize she was lying facedown on the bed, her naked body completely uncovered. In spite of the fact Ross had seen her nude before, somehow she felt more exposed as she considered Ross in his role as a pirate captain, seeing his captive sex slave for the first time.

She adopted a frightened tone, mimicking her own heroine. "Please, Captain, I beg of you. Don't hurt me."

Ross's hand came down hard on her bare ass. "I have not given you permission to speak," he shouted, so loudly Julia began to shake in earnest.

"It is time, madam, you learned your place here." Grabbing her hips, Ross pulled upwards. "Bend your legs and put them under you."

Doing as he commanded only earned her a harder spanking. "Open your legs," he yelled. "I am now your master and you will always keep yourself open to me. I always want your pussy and ass in clear view. Do you understand?"

"Y-yes sir," she stuttered, the intensity of the moment, of the fantasy, almost driving her to climax. Clearly, Ross was embellishing the plot—adding an erotic dimension Julia couldn't anticipate or resist.

Behind her, Ross didn't try to hide his grin. How much the fantasy was exciting her was evident in the tremors shaking her body. He knew Julia would love role-playing in bed. She'd spent the last ten years acting out her own romantic fantasies on paper. Now Ross would give her a chance to experience them for real, with his own desires added in to spice things up. The main benefit in acting out some of her stories was the fact that many of his own fantasies seemed to be tied directly to hers. Dominating her in bed, seeing her tied up and helpless, his to command in all things, was by far the most exhilarating moment of his life.

"Whenever I enter this cabin, you will stop what you are doing and throw yourself prostrate at my feet, facing away from me in just this manner. Do you understand?"

"Yes sir," she replied, her voice taking on a husky sound

that drove him crazy. The image of her on the bed, hands tied above her head, with her ass in the air and open to his view was one he was certain to take with him to his grave.

"Your clothing has been disposed of," he added.

"What?" she asked, fully enmeshed in her role.

He slapped her ass hard three times, leaving the flesh hot and red.

"Are you questioning your master?" he asked roughly.

"No," she whispered.

"No what?" he demanded.

"No sir."

"Have you ever had a man?" he asked gruffly, reaching out to prod at her wet entrance with rough fingers.

"N-no sir," she replied. Then bravely, adding in character, "Please, sir, I am a lady. I must save myself for my husband and my wedding night."

He met her comment with another spanking, this one harder than all the rest. The sight of Julia's gorgeous backside, red from his hand, compelled him to continue fulfilling his own dark needs—the fact she was playing along and not shying away left him rock hard. The opening of her body dripped with her undeniable desire.

"There will be no husband," he growled. "And your wedding night is tonight. This will hurt, my little virgin," he added harshly as he placed his erection at the opening of her wet pussy.

"Some day," he continued, "you will beg me for what I am about to give you." With that, he slammed into her, entering her completely in one powerful thrust. Julia's screams of rapture and the tight clamping of her cunt drove him on. No longer mindful of the fantasy, Ross pounded into her accepting body as if his only salvation lay at the end. Julia, delirious with passion, began to climax almost immediately, but Ross merely continued to lay siege to her body. Giving her no reprieve, he continued his sweet assault until Julia's orgasms began to hit her one after another, without cease, without mercy, until finally Ross let her take him overboard with her.

Several minutes passed before either of them came back to earth. Ross grimaced as he realized he'd collapsed on top of his tiny love.

"Sorry," he muttered, moving over to lie beside her. Reaching up, he released the ties holding her hands, gently massaging her sore shoulders.

No sooner had he released her from her bonds than Julia threw her arms around his neck, kissing him as if he'd given her all the gold in Fort Knox.

"Ross," she sighed, still breathless, "that was incredible. Amazing. I've never, I mean, I never knew—" She struggled for the right words, but Ross stopped her by simply saying, "Me either."

"Can we do it again?" she asked, looking so much like a child begging for a puppy that Ross burst into laughter.

"Right now?" he asked with a shake of his head. "Jesus, Jules, it'll take me a year to build up enough strength to just leave this bed, let alone love you like that again."

Julia grinned. "I wouldn't mind spending a year in this bed with you."

"You," he said, lightly kissing her nose, "will most definitely be the death of me. Go to sleep, angel."

Snuggling into his arms, Julia didn't need to be told twice. Ross suspected she was asleep before her head hit his shoulder. Gathering her tightly against him, he too succumbed to the deep slumber of a man well and truly satisfied.

Chapter Five

The smell and sound of bacon frying permeated the air, waking Julia from a sound sleep. Breathing deeply, she slowly opened her eyes, shocked, yet delighted by the image she saw. Ross was completely naked, except for an apron, cooking her breakfast. She had a perfect view of his bare buttocks and muscular back and she took advantage of it, admiring the scenery.

Faint scratch marks decorated both and she blushed recalling how they got there. She never would have guessed sex could be so exciting, so exhilarating, so amazing. She'd dreamed of sleeping with Ross about a million times, but no fantasy could even come close to the reality of last night. Now all she had to do was figure out where to go from here. *I had sex with Ross*, she repeated over and over in her mind, as if the entire thought were too preposterous to be believed. Her memories of the night flashed from remembered bliss to embarrassment to downright remorse. "How could I?" she muttered.

Without turning, Ross said, "You may as well forget attempting to back out of this one."

"W-what?" she asked, amazed he could be so in tune with her thoughts.

Loading two plates with food, he still didn't look at her.

"You're trying to figure out how to salvage a friendship that's not in danger. I can hear the gears in your mind churning from here."

Glancing over his shoulder, he gave her a drop-dead-gorgeous grin. "I told you last night. We're doing serious research and I haven't even begun to do all the things I've planned to do to you, so get your sweet ass outta that bed and come eat."

Julia caught her jaw before it fell completely open at the image his words evoked. Looking around the bed, she attempted to keep herself covered up with the sheet while trying to locate her robe. It was gone.

"Uh-uh." Ross shook his head as he watched her attempt at modesty. "No more clothes."

"What?" Julia cried. "If you think I'm going to parade around this freezing cabin without anything on, you're crazy."

"It's not freezing." Ross gestured to his own state of near undress. "I've cranked up the heat and built up the fire. If it gets much hotter in here, we're going to have to open a window. Come on, Brown Eyes, I saw it all last night and the food's getting cold." With that, he removed the apron and took his own place at the table, acting as if it were perfectly normal to be eating bacon and eggs in the nude.

Julia's rumbling stomach won in the battle against her modesty as she slowly lowered the quilt and climbed off the huge bed. She kept her eyes averted as she made her way to the table, nearly stumbling over the chair in her efforts to rapidly sit and cover her lap with a napkin.

Ross's deep chuckle across the table raised her gaze and her temper at the same time.

"I want my robe," she demanded.

"I want you," he answered easily, seemingly immune to her

anger.

Taken aback by the intense desire she saw in his eyes, Julia bit off her next remark and slowly picked up her fork.

Smiling at her acquiescence, Ross started to devour the huge pile of eggs on his plate like a starving man. The two of them ate in relative silence, although Julia could sense Ross's gaze on her through most of the meal. She wasn't used to being with such a virile man—one who made no bones about his desires and who wasn't afraid to take what he wanted. The men in her past had been gentle as lambs, often letting her dictate how the relationship progressed. She felt out of her element with Ross, a man clearly used to being in charge. Quite frankly, she was surprised by how much she enjoyed his controlling presence. She'd always considered herself a modern, independent woman who had no use for a man in her life. Who could have guessed she'd actually enjoy being ordered around in the bedroom?

The only problem she could see was facing what would happen when they left this cabin. The fact was she *was* an independent woman, one who refused to let herself be swept away in an ill-fated romance, especially to a man like Ross who was clearly a bad bet. The last ten years as his best friend had proven to her he was unable to commit to any woman—and if she was being completely honest with herself, she was an even worse bet. She didn't want a relationship. Her heart couldn't take losing someone she loved again. It had taken her years to recover from the loss of her parents. Hell, even the mere thought of Duke's death still tore her apart and he had been only a cat. What would happen if she gave her heart to Ross and if, in his typical fashion, he broke it?

"Oh no," he said lightly, as he finished the last piece of toast on his plate.

"Is something wrong?" She noticed her own plate was still full of food.

"You're thinking again. Jules, what do I have to say to make you understand this is okay? You and I—together like this. Hell, woman, it's more than okay. It's about damn time! Enough of this second-guessing and worrying. Trust me. Please."

His voice was so earnest and his eyes so consoling, Julia felt her fears slipping away from her as easily as her clothing had last night. She did trust Ross and she wanted very much to continue "researching" with him. She would put her fears and worries aside and live for the moment. Taking a deep breath, she smiled for the first time since waking up, relinquishing the reins to Ross. Truth be told, she couldn't wait to see what he had planned next.

"Okay, Mr. Phillips," she teased. "You win. Big surprise there. Have you ever lost at anything?"

Grinning, Ross stood and walked around the table to where she sat.

"Nothing that really mattered," he answered, kneeling beside her. "Now, Brown Eyes, how about actually eating that food, rather than pushing it around the plate?" He winked at her. "You're going to need your strength later on."

Picking up her fork, he slowly fed her nearly everything on the plate until she finally pushed the dish away. "Enough or I won't be able to get up from the table. Hey," she said, sudden realization dawning, "I didn't know you could cook."

"Just breakfast—bacon and scrambled eggs, Jules. And, sadly, I didn't bring enough of that for every meal. Looks like we're going to have to stumble our way through the rest of the meals."

"I don't suppose anyone delivers pizza all the way up here," she added.

"No. Not that anyone could get a car up here in that blizzard if they did." He gestured as they walked toward the window.

"Oh no," she cried as she squinted against the brightness of the thick blanket of snow covering the ground. "We're going to be stuck up here for days." Glancing up at the cloud-covered sky, she groaned. The snow was still falling in fat flakes, burying the porch of the cabin in deep drifts. "Maybe even weeks."

Strong arms engulfed her as Ross's lips grazed her ear. "I can think of worse things," he whispered.

"But won't you get in trouble if you aren't back at work?" Her heart raced as his hands left her waist, climbing up to loosely cup her breasts.

"I own the company, Jules. I can come and go as I please. I told Max where I was going and that I might be gone for a while. He can hold down the fort until I return." As he spoke, his fingers toyed with her nipples until they were both pebbled hard and incredibly sensitive. Each time he brushed the tips, she felt the moisture between her legs increase until she squirmed to catch wayward drops that started sliding down her inner thigh.

"Ross," she whispered, half protest, half plea.

"Ross, what?" His lips grazed the sensitive area at the nape of her neck as his fingers continued their magic on her breasts. Julia quivered at the sensations he aroused, until she surprised herself by responding to his question.

"More," she demanded.

"Lean forward," he whispered. She remained motionless, unsure what he meant until his hand left her breast to begin pushing gently at her back. Before she realized his intent, she felt her hard nipples pressed against the ice-cold glass of the window. Gasping, she attempted to break away from his firm but insistent grip.

"It's cold."

"Think how good it will feel when I warm them up again," he replied, not releasing her.

"Ross—"

"Beg me."

"What?" she asked, uncertain she'd heard his terse order correctly.

"Beg me. Beg me for what you want."

"But—"

Ross pushed her harder against the glass, no longer chilling her nipples, but her entire breasts.

"Tell me what you want, Brown Eyes."

"Let me loose," she pleaded, no longer able to control the demands her body was making. "Take me in your mouth. Suck me hard. Make me hot again." Still Ross didn't release her. "Please!"

Suddenly, his hand at her back was gone. Julia turned slowly in his arms. Raising her hands to his shoulders and then to his hair, she pulled his mouth down to hers for a kiss. A kiss she commanded and controlled, her lips hard against his own as she insisted upon entry, her tongue finding its way into the heat of his mouth. While Julia directed the kiss, Ross took possession of her body. Swiveling, he backed her up to the bed. As soon as the back of her thighs touched the high mattress, he pushed her down, spreading her legs to stand between them.

Bending down, Ross gave Julia everything she'd demanded and more as he took first one breast and then the other into his mouth. Laving them with his hot tongue, nipping them with his teeth, he warmed her up to boiling in a matter of minutes.

Mari Carr

Julia attempted to wrap her legs around his waist to pull him closer, but Ross, wise to that trick, refused to relinquish his control. Grabbing her ankles, he stepped away from the bed, looking down at her.

"Not yet, Brown Eyes," he said tenderly. "I want you to do something for me first."

Confused, Julia slowly rose up onto her elbows, shocked at how she no longer minded her nudity in Ross's presence, her own body betraying her modesty in its clamoring for release.

"What?"

"Sit in the center of the bed and prop yourself up on those pillows." He walked to the bottom of the bed.

Intrigued, Julia did as he asked, taking note of the imperiousness of his command. His voice brought back memories of his pirate captain from the night before and she squirmed, uncomfortably aroused.

"Spread your legs," he demanded harshly.

Julia started to protest his tone, but he stopped her. "You will not speak, Jules. Only do as I say." Then to soften his words, he winked.

Smiling, Julia remembered his earlier words, *"trust me"*, and she slowly opened her legs, aware of the view she was giving him of her wet pussy.

"Last night was your first orgasm." He shook his head, clearly disappointed for some reason. "Julia, I'm not always going to be around when you feel these sexual urges. I'm not sure how you've lived as long as you have, alone and unable to take care of your own needs. So, I'm going to show you how."

Her jaw dropped open at his words, but none of her own would come. Before she could even consider her response to his brazen suggestion, he continued, "I want you to do exactly what

I tell you. No talking, Jules, only feeling. You will like this." She sensed he could see her hands shaking slightly. "I promise."

When she began to close her legs again, he harshly added, "Keep your legs open." When she failed to extend them far enough, he reached over the end of the bed and pulled her ankles until she was fully spread apart.

"Move your hands to your breasts," he said softly. "You have the most amazing tits, so sensitive and full. Touch them like I was earlier, by the window. Cup them." His voice was quiet now, almost hypnotic and in spite of her reservations Julia felt her hands responding to his directions.

"That's it," he continued. "Now pinch your nipples. Not too rough at first. Gradually build up the pressure on them. Feel how hard they are. Roll them around a bit. Good girl."

Julia felt trapped by his stare, enthralled by his words, and she knew he was enjoying her actions as much as she was. Her gaze fell to his erection. Noticing her look, Ross slowly took his own hard penis in his hand, rubbing it from root to tip over and over, the movement mesmerizing her.

"Bend your head over a little," he added hoarsely. "Use your tongue on that poor hard nipple. It wants more attention. That's it. Now suck it into your mouth."

Julia moaned slightly at the feeling of her own breast in her mouth, her tongue teasing the nipple until she thought she would explode from the pressure.

"God, you have no idea how hot that looks. Not all women are large enough to do that," Ross praised. "Don't forget the other one. It's lonely too."

Moving her lips to her other nipple, Julia squirmed again, desperate for Ross to come inside her. She felt ready to beg him when he asked, "You need more, don't you?"

Groaning with relief, Julia nodded, expecting him to crawl

onto the bed. However, he kept speaking. "Move your right hand down, over your stomach. Run your fingers through the soft hair down there and play with that sweet little nub."

"Ross," Julia cried, the touch of her fingers on her own pussy driving her wild.

"That's right." He leaned closer to where her fingers were moving. "Pretend it's me. Imagine it's my fingers playing with you. Your hot cunt is mine from now on. Only mine. What do you want my fingers to do now, Jules?"

"In-inside me," she panted.

"Then put them inside." He moved slightly closer, until Julia imagined she could feel his breath on her wet pussy.

Slowly, she dragged her fingers down over her clit, inching them even closer to her own soaking entry.

"So wet," he purred. "So hot and wet. Can you feel that, Jules? You're on fire, aren't you?"

"Y-yes."

"You aren't pretending, Jules," he said tightly. "Remember it's my hand inside you and I would never touch you so lightly. You're a wildcat. You like it rough. Move your hand, Jules." His voice rose. "Faster! Harder! Put in another finger. And another one. Dammit, Jules, use your thumb, rub your clit. More! Now, come."

At his last shouted order, she felt herself shatter into a million tiny pieces. The room went dark as she silently screamed out his name.

Ross watched in amazement as his gorgeous writer writhed in delight and ecstasy. He knew how powerful words were in her mind, but to see her succumb so totally to his commands overwhelmed his own senses and he felt the last of his control slip completely away.

She had only begun to come down from her orgasm when Ross crawled onto the bed and entered her fully with one push. The power, the dominance of the motion sent Julia immediately back over the edge and she screamed aloud this time as another orgasm took her. The tight convulsions of her pussy grabbed Ross like a fist, provoking his own explosive climax in just three thrusts.

They came back down to earth together and Ross realized he had collapsed on top of her once again. Julia was struggling for breath and laughing as they parted, Ross falling to his side, pulling her with him. He silently rejoiced as he felt her once again curl into his chest, her soft hair, damp with perspiration, covering him like a blanket.

"How did I do?" she asked softly, after a few moments.

"Do?" His brain was still a jumble after the most incredible climax of his life.

"With my masturbation lesson?" She giggled lightly. "That was the next phase of the research, wasn't it?"

Damn the research. Did she seriously think this was just a game? He was coming like an untried schoolboy every time he got inside her. Every time he left her body, he felt an unceasing yearning to get right back in. How the hell could she honestly believe this was simply a snowy afternoon's entertainment?

Shaking himself, he looked over her head to see the snow still falling. He had time. By the looks of the weather, lots of it. He'd keep to the plan. If she wanted to keep researching, that's what they'd do. Soon, he'd have her so ensnared in his web of desire and passion, she'd never want to leave. God—he hoped so, anyway. He no longer had any doubt that Jules was his soul mate.

"Yeah, it was, and you did great, Brown Eyes. Just great."

Chapter Six

Ross awoke several hours later to the sound of fingers tapping a keyboard at a frantic pace. Glancing over, he saw Julia, just as he'd seen her a thousand times in the past, one leg bent beneath her as the images in her mind flew through her fingers to the screen in front of her. The only difference was this time, rather than wearing her usual fleece pants and long-sleeved T-shirt, she was draped only in a blanket. A blanket that, fortunately for him, had been forgotten as it lay around her waist, leaving her breasts bare. A glass of iced tea sat untouched beside her as she focused on the pages before her.

How much of what she wrote was derived from their researching? The last forty-eight hours had been the most exhilarating and exhausting of his life and, for the first time since he'd become her editor nearly a decade ago, he found himself overwhelmed with curiosity over what she was writing. Ross had never had any trouble waiting until the final manuscript to see her work. Julia was an extremely talented writer. She would make her plot proposal, he'd tweak it, then he'd simply wait while she worked her magic. He found himself almost desperate to see what she thought of their explorations during the past twenty-four hours. To see if she was as heady from the experience as he was.

"Well, well, well," he said, when he couldn't stand the

suspense any longer. "Looks like you've broken through the writer's block. That is your erotic-romance novel you're tapping away at, isn't it?"

Her instant blush answered his question and he suspected she was indeed putting some, if not all, of their actions into words.

"Want me to take a look, see if you need to do any tweaking?" he asked nonchalantly. He rose from the bed to cross the room to where she sat at the desk.

"No," she said quickly, saving and exiting from the file. "Not until I'm finished. You know that."

"Well," Ross teased, "I thought since we were collaborating on this project, you might want me to take a more hands-on approach."

"More hands-on than what you've been doing? I don't think I can handle any more of your hands!"

Delighted with her jest, Ross bent down and impulsively placed a quick kiss to the end of her nose. "Don't let me interrupt your creative flow. I'll just be over here in the kitchen, slaving over your lunch."

"Actually," she said, "I was about to take a break. I'll help you. I think there are sandwich fixings in the fridge. Even we can handle that."

"Sounds good," he replied, grabbing sliced turkey, lettuce, tomatoes, mayo and some leftover bacon from the refrigerator. "If you look in that cabinet by the sink, I think there's a big bag of potato chips."

Together they made and devoured their lunch, washing the sandwiches down with ice-cold soda and talking about insignificant things—people at the publishing company, the weather, the latest episode of CSI.

"I suppose I should get back to work," Julia said as they washed off their lunch plates. "I did come up here to write a book."

"Yeah, well," Ross began, "I know you hate distractions while you're working. Tell you what. I think I'll go tackle some of that snow with a shovel."

"But it's still snowing."

"Yep, but it's probably better to attack it in small increments or I'll never be able to find my way back to the woodpile. I'd hate for the heat to go out and us to be digging through three feet of snow looking for firewood. Besides, you know me. I can't stand to be stuck inside with nothing to do."

Julia's cheeks flushed red as she glanced toward the bed, betraying her thoughts.

"Besides that. Dammit woman, but if you don't stop looking at me like that, you will be the death of me! Have mercy on an old man!"

She grinned at his comment. "You're only thirty-five."

"And feeling every minute of it. Oh, what I wouldn't give to be twenty years old right now."

Fifteen minutes later, Julia glanced out the window to admire the strength in Ross's arms and back as he easily shoveled the heavy snow off the path leading from the cabin to the woodpile.

Sighing, she silently chastised herself for actually missing him. "My God," she whispered, "he's only thirty feet away! Get it together, Julia."

It would do her absolutely no good to become romantically infatuated with Ross. He was a confirmed bachelor, a love-'em-and-leave-'em kind of guy. She had to keep that thought in her head before she found herself giving him something she swore she'd never give anyone—her heart.

The rest of the day passed in quiet solitude. They both decided since clothing was a necessity for working in the snow, she should also be allowed to cover up. Ross gave his grumbling consent and allowed Julia to put on her work outfit—the warm fleece lounge pants and a T-shirt. He came in twice to add more wood to the pile inside the cabin and warm his numb fingers around the steaming cups of hot chocolate Julia made, before venturing back out into the freezing elements. Unfortunately, the path he'd shoveled was already covered again with a thin crust of snow.

After dinner, they lay together once again on the soft bearskin rug. Ross put a CD in the player and the soft sounds of Tom Waits's album *Closing Time* started lulling them peacefully toward sleep.

Ross broke the silence by finally asking her the question she'd been waiting for all afternoon. "How's the writing coming?"

"Fine," she answered. For the first time in her life, she found her words failing her. Fact was, all she'd done was put together a diary of sorts. She knew she should be developing her characters and plot, but instead all she could do whenever she sat in front of the computer was recollect the power of Ross's touch, the incredible feeling of him as he thrust deep inside her, the magic of each orgasm he'd given her. What would he think if he knew she'd spent nearly two hours this afternoon merely describing every feature, every nuance of his body in minute detail?

"Need to do more research?" he asked mischievously.

"Perhaps. What did you have in mind?"

"Have you ever given a man a blowjob?"

Red-hot embarrassment raced through her body. Just

when she thought he couldn't shock her anymore.

"Well, I—I mean, I—" she stammered. "Oh hell, no, but I've always wanted to."

The silence in the cabin was rocked by Ross's spontaneous laughter.

Hurt by his response, Julia started to rise. She had told him she wasn't very experienced, but she didn't need him to ridicule her for it.

"No," he said, grabbing her shoulders and pulling her back down to him. "I'm not laughing at you. Christ, Jules, you have no idea, do you?"

"I told you before I didn't. Now let me go. This isn't funny."

"That's not what I meant," Ross replied. "I didn't mean to hurt your feelings. I know you're inexperienced and I don't think that's funny. Hell, it's a crime. A sexy woman like you. No, what I meant is you have no idea how adorable you are. After all that we've done, the fact that you can still blush like a teenager when I ask a simple question—"

"A simple question? You use the term 'blowjob' in a sentence like it's a commonplace topic of conversation."

"You're writing an erotic novel. It better become comfortable dialogue to you as well. Besides, I wish you'd told me about this deep, dark desire of yours to give a blowjob. I would've been happy to oblige you years ago."

Julia acknowledged Ross's jest for what it was—harmless— and smiled at him. Besides, he'd called her sexy and adorable— all in the same breath.

"Who said I wanted to give one to you?" she asked, enjoying the image of his humor suddenly turning to offense. She could tease him as easily as he did her.

"And who in the hell's cock have you been fantasizing

about sucking?"

"Jealous?" she teased, wishing for a moment he truly was.

"Maybe." He pulled her face to his for a rough kiss that quickly turned heated, and for a moment, Julia wondered if perhaps he really was jealous. His kiss was potent and his hands fiercely possessive as he frantically pulled her shirt over her head.

"Too many clothes," he murmured. He yanked her pants off with even less finesse and Julia felt giddy with the knowledge that he seemed to lose all control when it came to her. "I knew it was a mistake to let you cover up."

Only when she was totally naked in his arms did he seem to regain his composure. "That's better." His gaze devoured her once more.

"For you maybe," she whispered, gesturing to his fully clad body.

Grinning, Ross tackled the buttons on his jeans as Julia went to work on the ones on his flannel shirt. Twice they bumped heads in their haste to divest him of his clothing. Finally, after much struggling and laughter, they were both naked and incredibly aroused.

Kissing her again, Ross's lips became soft, almost worshipful as he slowly tantalized her mouth with his own and her body with his exploring hands.

Julia's hands mimicked the actions of his as she too studied and caressed his body. When she reached his rock-hard arousal, she used both hands, first gently, then more firmly, stroking down and reaching underneath to tease his balls with her fingers, before moving back up again. Tiny liquid drops escaped the end and Julia licked her lips, wondering what he would taste like. Without awaiting an invitation, she bent down and ran her tongue around the head of his penis, teasing the small slit with just the tip of her tongue.

Several breathless curses fell from his lips and Ross grasped her head. "God, Brown Eyes," he moaned, "do that again."

Smiling, she complied, kneeling before him and licking him several more times all around his firm hard-on before finally taking him fully into her mouth. She worried she had hurt him when she heard his sharp intake of breath, but then all uncertainty left her as she felt his grip on her head tighten as he pushed her farther down on his cock—silently begging for more.

His shaking hands and harsh breathing gave her clues as to when he enjoyed what she was doing. She experimented with her teeth and her tongue, applying pressure to different spots, discovering what he liked and what he didn't. She was amazed to discover how much she enjoyed doing this. The smell and taste of him was so uniquely Ross. She felt as if she'd been given a small peek at a part of him others could never see.

"Jules," he said after several more minutes, "sweetheart, I'm going to come. If you don't want—" But Julia cut off the rest of his words by sucking him even harder and farther into her mouth.

"Oh shit," he cried as his climax overtook him, great spurts of cum sliding down Julia's throat, all of which she drank greedily, refusing to release him until the last drop erupted.

Ross's grip on her head relaxed and, as a great oak falls in the woods, he collapsed onto the rug as if dead. Scrambling up, Julia knelt beside him, suddenly concerned.

"Ross, are you all right?"

"No," he mumbled, "I was right. You killed me."

"What?" She bent down to check his heart. It was racing and she became worried. What if he was having a heart attack?

After all, he'd warned her earlier he wasn't young anymore.

Noticing her concern, Ross grabbed her, pulling her on top of him. "I'm kidding, Brown Eyes."

"Kidding?" She slugged him lightly on the shoulder. "Dammit, Ross, don't tease me like that. I thought you were having a heart attack."

"Too many more blowjobs like that and I might. I thought you said you've never done that."

"I haven't," she responded, pleased by his reaction. "I've just thought about it."

"Lord, save me from sexy female writers because that is one hell of an active imagination you have there."

"Glad you liked it," she replied.

"Yeah, well, never let it be said I failed to reciprocate." He sat up slowly. "There's a backpack over there on that chair, Jules." He gestured to an easy chair by the bed. "If I could move, I'd go get it. Mind fetching it for me? I've got some treats in there for you."

"Chocolate treats?"

"No, you naughty imp, better than chocolate."

She raised her eyebrows, suspicious about his remark, but went to get the bag. Dropping to her knees beside him, she placed it in his lap. "What's in it?"

"Toys."

"Aren't we a little old for toys?" she teased uneasily, suddenly aware of what he probably considered treats.

"Don't look at me like that," he said. "You know I won't hurt you."

"So there aren't whips and chains and other instruments of torture in there?" Her tone was light, but she knew Ross could sense her trepidation.

"Of course not, Jules. I'm not into pain and unless we discover that you are, we won't play those games." His answer was straightforward and honest and Julia silently sighed a breath of relief.

"I don't like pain either," she said, before recalling Ross's spankings and the pleasure she derived from them. "I mean, I don't think I do."

Grinning, Ross pulled her onto his lap. "A little spanking isn't exactly the same thing as S & M, sweetheart."

"So, what's in the bag?" she asked, curiosity getting the best of her.

"Ah, getting into the research now, I see."

"Ross," she repeated impatiently, "what's in the bag?"

Opening it, but shielding the contents from her, Ross rummaged through until he found what he was looking for. Ross pulled the items out and Julia had to suppress her gasp of surprise and uneasiness. He held them out to her for her inspection.

"Is that what I think it is?" she asked nervously, trying to wiggle out of his grasp. Although she'd read about butt plugs, she'd never actually seen one.

Ross dropped the items on the rug and pulled her more firmly onto his lap. "Jules," he consoled. "Honey, if you hate it, we'll stop."

"If it hurts—" She bit her lower lip.

"We'll stop. Trust me?" he repeated and she nodded.

Kissing her gently, he soothed her fears with his sweet ministrations—rubbing her back, running his fingers through her hair, tickling her feet. He rose slowly, then bent down to lift her before carrying her to the bed. He joined her then pulled the covers over them both.

"What about the—" She gestured to his backpack.

"Later," he whispered. "Right now, all I want is you."

And he proved his words with each caress, each kiss, each orgasm. They fell asleep wrapped in each other's arms and Julia realized as she drifted off she'd never felt so loved. If she'd been less tired, the thought would have scared the hell out of her, but instead, in her exhausted state, she allowed herself to pretend, just for the night, that Ross did love her and they would beat all the odds stacked against them to live a long, happy life together.

Chapter Seven

It was still dark outside when Julia awoke. She sensed Ross was also awake, then realized what had roused her. She was on her stomach and Ross was kissing a path down her back, his tongue darting out now and then for a taste of her. She could get used to these late-night adventures.

Tensing slightly, she felt his hands on her buttocks, but she relaxed as he began to softly massage them. Every touch felt like heaven and she wondered how she would ever be able to return to the real world—with Ross, the friend, instead of Ross, the lover. The snow had stopped earlier in the day and the weather forecast called for warmer days ahead. With the melting snow, Julia began to feel as if her days with Ross here in her own private Eden were numbered.

"Bend your knees," he said, lightly pushing her up. She was still drowsy and so satiated by his earlier loving that the sudden, unexpected feeling of cold gel on her anus caused her to jerk.

"Hush," he soothed, "it'll warm up in a second." True to his word, the gel did seem to heat up as he slowly rubbed it around her back entrance.

"God, angel," he whispered, "I want you so bad. Every time I come inside you, I leave you only to want to get right back in."

His words, as always, affected her strongly and she began

to push back toward his hand, silently asking for more.

As he applied more gel, she felt his finger seeking entrance to the dark portal. No one had ever breached her ass and she was surprised by the intensity of the sensations provoked by merely the tip of his finger. Slowly, he worked his finger in deeper and soon she felt herself pushing back against him, seeking more.

"That's it, sweetheart. Let me in." He removed one finger only to return with two.

She gasped for breath as the pressure of his two fingers increased, becoming painful. "Push against me," he instructed.

She attempted to do as he asked, trying to decide if she liked his actions or not. It hurt, but not unbearably, and she had to admit there was some part of her that was deeply turned on by his wicked touch. Determined to learn all she could, she relaxed until he had both fingers buried completely within her.

"Christ, you're tight," he said, starting to thrust his fingers in the rhythm she'd come to love.

Arching back against him, she followed his movements, the pain decreasing as the pleasure grew.

"Ross," she cried as the stimulation became too much, "more, please."

Rather than giving her more, however, his fingers left her completely. She started to protest.

"Wait," he murmured, his lips grazing her ear, his tongue darting out to tease her earlobe.

Suddenly she felt something hard pressing into her. She started to pull away, but Ross's strong arm across her shoulders held her firmly in place. She felt him put the tip of the tube of lubrication to her anus as more of the sticky gel permeated her tight hole. Then he began to press the plug into her. A butt plug, she thought, recalling the instrument she'd seen him pull out of the backpack earlier. She'd read about them, but she never imagined in her wildest fantasies he would ever want to put one inside her. She understood the implication. The plug would gradually loosen the muscles of her anus and it would make it easier for Ross to fuck her there. He wanted to fuck her ass. The thought should frighten her, but instead she struggled to take the plug. She wanted him there. God, she wanted him anywhere she could get him. What kind of wanton woman had she become? What was he doing to her?

"Almost there," he whispered, gently guiding the plug until she was filled completely. Once he finished, he soothingly massaged her buttocks again.

"Lie back down," he said, pushing her lightly on the bed. She struggled to accommodate the large plug inside her, feeling more than a little uncomfortable.

Once he had her tucked back up against him, he asked, "Are you okay?" with such concern, Jules felt her heart swell.

"I'm fine," she whispered hoarsely. "Ross," she started to say, words failing her.

"What, Brown Eyes?" He kissed the top of her head.

"Do men like that? I mean—being with women that way?" she asked, suddenly very afraid Ross would think less of her for allowing him to do such an unspeakable thing to her.

He tipped her face up to his with his finger on her chin. "I can't speak for all men, but I find I want you every way a man can have a woman, Jules. It may seem primitive or uncivilized, but I don't think I'll be able to rest until I've possessed every part of you—your mouth, your pussy, your ass, all of you. You've lit a fire in my soul and it feels like it will consume me if I don't quench it. Does that make any sense?" His eyes filled with apprehension.

"Yes," she whispered, lightly kissing his lips, "it does. I feel exactly the same way."

He smiled, returning her light kiss. "Can you sleep? With it inside you?"

She nodded shyly. "Yes."

"Good," he replied lightly, the real Ross reappearing, "because I don't think I can wait much longer to have you there. I don't want to hurt you and this will help. Have I told you lately how incredible you are?"

"Not in the last couple of hours," she teased.

"You're incredible," he said, so seriously she was stunned for a moment. "Go to sleep, Brown Eyes. Busy day tomorrow. Research, research, research."

ဆ

The morning sun temporarily blinded Julia as she attempted to open her eyes. She knew before she did so that she was alone in the bed. She started to sit up, forgetting about the large plug still buried deep inside her.

"Oh," she cried.

Her distress brought Ross running from the bathroom, a towel wrapped low on his hips, half his face covered in shaving cream.

"What's wrong?" He quickly crossed the room to help her.

"Nothing," she said, too humiliated to actually say the words.

"I heard you cry out. Are you hurt?"

"No. I just forgot—" she waved her hands around, hoping he would understand the meaningless gesture, "—you know. I sat up too fast."

Grinning, Ross bent down and kissed her, covering her with at least half of the shaving cream on his face.

"Hey!" she complained.

"I'll take care of you in a minute." He laughed at her foamy face. "Let me finish shaving first. Actually, why don't you join me? I want to shave you as well."

"Thanks for the invitation." She wiped the foam off her face. "But believe it or not, under all this shaving cream, I have no facial hair."

"I didn't mean I'd shave your face," he replied, obviously pleased by the blushes he managed to evoke with just a few words.

"Oh." She was stunned by his suggestion.

"Come on." He took her hand and pulled her to the bathroom. "First we need to get that plug out of you and then we'll discuss the shaving."

∞

Forty-five minutes later, Julia found herself showered and free of not only the plug, but her pubic hair as well. "How do I let you talk me into these things?" she muttered, pulling her terry cloth robe around her and running a comb through her freshly washed hair.

Ross grabbed her from behind to envelop her in a big bear hug, obviously delighted with his morning's work. "Face it, Jules," he joked, taking the comb from her hand and throwing it on the desk, "underneath that prim exterior, you're as big a sex maniac as me."

"God forbid," she replied with mock seriousness as she leaned back into his warm embrace. "What's for breakfast?"

"You," he answered and before she could reply, he lifted her up and carried her over to the kitchen table.

She giggled as he laid her facedown on the cool wood, then she noticed the scarves he had tied to the legs. "Ross," she said, trying to wiggle off the flat surface.

"That's master to you, slave." His voice once again took on its imperious tone. "I paid good money for you from the slave traders and I expect you will make a welcome addition to my harem. But first," he added, a strong hand on her back holding her in place, "I must see to your bondage." Ross managed to tie her arms straight above her head with relative ease considering the fact, catching on quickly to his fantasy, she had begun to seriously struggle for freedom.

"That's right, slave." He roughly pulled her hair back to give him access to her face. "Fight me. It will make it so much more satisfying when I break your will."

"I'll never submit," she cried, getting into the spirit of their game, kicking away from him as best she could.

The way he tied her arms kept the upper part of her body horizontal across the tabletop, while her hips and legs lay vertical over the edge. Gripping her feet, Ross proceeded to tie each ankle to a different corner leg on the table, leaving her ass and pussy open for his wandering hands, which seemed to continually caress her newly bared mons and ass impersonally as if truly inspecting his purchased goods.

"A feast fit for the gods," he proclaimed when he had her securely tied. "My servants have prepared you well for me. And now, we begin your training. This cunt," he said, touching her roughly, "is mine. If I choose to offer you to my soldiers as a prize, you will allow them access to it. Whenever I want to taste it, you will offer it to me. And your orgasms belong to me. Only at my permission will you come." With this, he knelt between her legs and showed his appreciation for her rich bounty, his tongue parting her wet folds to plunge inside.

"Never," she cried, secretly enjoying his invasion of her body.

"Soon, slave," he said roughly, "soon, you will beg."

His knots proved well tied in spite of Julia's attempts to set herself free and attack her attacker. Not out of anger at the bondage, but out of anger at his teasing touches. He kept her poised on the edge of an orgasm for close to an hour, proving his words true—she was at his mercy and she would beg. Each time she felt herself falling off the pinnacle he backed away, bringing her down with too-soft touches that merely dampened the fire within her rather than stoking it to a roaring blaze. Amused by her continual verbal abuse, Ross refused to be baited, refused to break character, and Julia felt sure she would kill him when he freed her. Each of her curses was met with more sensual torture. Soon, Julia found herself begging for release as she called Ross master, promising to be a good slave at his request, promising him anything he wanted.

Apparently appeased by her surrender, Ross rose quickly and replaced his tongue with his fingers. Grateful for the sudden change, Julia choked back a sob, struggling desperately to impale herself more deeply on his thick digits, only to feel him pull away completely.

"You please me greatly, slave." As he spoke, he retrieved a vibrator he'd brought from his bag of tricks. Pushing it firmly into her dripping pussy, he savored her moans of pleasure.

"More," she cried, a mantra Ross was secretly coming to love as much as he loved her.

"No, slave," he said harshly. "It is I who commands you." Removing the small vibrator now covered with her body's juices, he slowly slipped it into her anus. When it was fully inserted, he turned it on low, listening to her cries of delight.

"You will not come until I say. If you disobey me in this, you will be punished severely. Do you understand?"

"Yes, master," she whimpered.

He watched her bite back a scream as he pulled a chair over and sat behind her, watching as she writhed helplessly, attempting to rub herself against the table.

"Please," she whispered, when he refused to move.

"Not yet. You must learn your place, slave. You belong to me." Reaching forward, he turned up the power on the vibrator and she began to tremble with the onslaught of an orgasm.

"If you come without permission, I will beat you."

Leaning back, he watched her desperate attempts to still the tremors in her body. Taking deep breaths, she seemed to be struggling against the oncoming climax. Once more, he increased the speed of the vibrator and she fought back a scream.

Sensing her distress, as well as his own overwhelming desire, he rose slowly. She whimpered as he approached the table.

"Good slave," he whispered. "You've done well." Slowly, he pushed his hard erection into her mouth, savoring the tightness of her lips as she drank greedily at his cock. Forcing himself to set a slow, steady pace, Ross continued to thrust as Julia's sobbing pleas teased his sensitive flesh. Sensing she couldn't take any more, he pulled out, demanding, "Now, slave, come."

The convulsions of her climax spurred him to further action as he removed the vibrator from her ass and pressed his cock in her wet pussy. His thrusts became faster and harder, each one moving the table across the room until it hit the kitchen cabinets, finally holding her still for his relentless assault. No sooner did her orgasm end before another began. He counted five before he felt his own climax erupting inside her, powerful jets of seed filling her womb. His cries mingled with hers, his sweat pouring down onto her damp body.

For several long moments neither of them moved, and Ross suspected Julia had actually lost consciousness for a few seconds. When he finally felt the strength returning to his limbs, he untied her arms and legs, helping her to the bed, where he massaged the tension of her bondage away.

She was nearly asleep when she mumbled something. Something that sounded very much to Ross like, "I love you, master."

Grinning like the Cheshire cat, Ross lightly kissed her sleeping face before whispering his reply, well aware she wouldn't remember her words or his when she awoke. "I love you too, Brown Eyes."

Chapter Eight

The next few days passed in a timeless sort of quality—Ross and Julia's newfound relationship thriving in a magical world of undeniable lust and exciting fantasies. Although neither of them had truly spoken the words aloud, Ross couldn't help but hope his love-scarred beauty was coming around. Each day they awoke to make love, followed by food, some light activity—usually him chopping wood and shoveling snow while she wrote—then more food and more sex. Although it hadn't snowed again, the blizzard had dropped at least a foot and a half of snow on the ground, leaving them completely stranded. Not that he was in a hurry to return to the real world.

Neither of them mentioned what would happen when they made their way back to New York. Ross attempted to bring up the subject a few times, but each time, Julia managed to change the topic. Unwilling to risk the rapport they'd built over the past week, Ross finally let the subject drop for good. His intentions toward her had not changed, but instead they had solidified to such a point that he felt certain he would not rest until he convinced her to marry him.

During the hours they spent out of bed, they talked about their lives, more deeply than they had in all their years as just friends. Ross told her about his childhood, growing up with four younger brothers and two very loving parents. Julia marveled that she'd never met any of Ross's family and he even surprised her by inviting her to a family reunion planned over Easter break.

Julia told him about her parents for the first time, even talking about the night they'd died. She'd never shared her thoughts, fears and feelings of that painful night with anyone and Ross held her as she cried, her emotions raw from the intensity of her revelations.

As they cuddled in front of the fire, Ross asked, "What's your ultimate sexual fantasy?"

Despite all they had shared together, Julia was still a bit shy regarding her sexuality and desires and Ross hoped to break her of that completely before they left the cabin. He wanted her to feel comfortable enough with him that she could share her innermost thoughts and hopes without trepidation or fear.

"Fantasy? I don't know," she answered after a few moments, although Ross could see she clearly did know.

"Tell me," he prodded. "Everyone has some deep, dark fantasy. Lord knows I've tried most of mine with you in the past week. What's yours?"

"I wouldn't say we've indulged all of yours," she answered, in what he suspected was an attempt to change the subject. Although she'd worn the butt plug for a couple of hours each day, they'd yet to have anal sex. Somehow the time had never seemed right. Ross sensed she was still slightly uneasy with the thought and he didn't want to rush her.

"Nice try," he replied, refusing to be put off. "We have plenty of time for everything I want to do to you. Tonight, I want to enact one of your fantasies."

"I can't tell you. It's too embarrassing. God knows what you'd think of me."

Shaking his head, Ross chuckled lightly. "What I'd think of you? My God, woman, I've tied you to the kitchen table and the bed, shaved your pussy and used numerous sex toys on you. I've been a pirate and a sultan. I've indulged in your mind-blowing blowjobs several times, while taking you missionary position, doggy style, and I've even had you ride me in a hot tub twice and you're worried about your fantasies affecting my feelings toward you!"

Laughing, Julia relented. "Fine, I'll tell you. It's not like we can do it anyway."

"Oh yeah?" Ross said, up to any challenge. "Try me."

"When I read those erotica books you loaned me, one of them talked about a woman who, well, who—" She paused.

"Who what?" Ross prodded.

"Had two men at one time," she stammered out so rapidly Ross wasn't sure he'd heard her correctly.

"Two men," he repeated as she blushed and looked away.

"It's silly, I know. Please forget I said anything."

"I would never share you," Ross said without thinking.

The seriousness of his tone took her aback. He clearly meant what he said. Uneasy with the conversation, Julia wished she could take back her words. "Well, it's not like there's another man here or even at home who wants me. It was a silly thought. Let's forget I said it. Okay?"

"No." Ross's eyes were still deeply disturbed. "You've obviously done more than simply consider it, but Jules, you're mine." His face was so determined she shuddered at the power behind his words.

"For now," she whispered, remembering that he'd made no promises for the future and likely never would. She refused to let herself fall into his spell any deeper than she already had.

"You're mine," he repeated, grasping her upper arms tightly in response to her softly spoken words. "Mine." The grip of his fingers digging into her arms was painful and Julia was shocked by the power behind his declaration.

However as soon as the words passed his lips, he masked his feelings. So quickly in fact, Julia wondered if they had ever been there.

"Ross," she whispered, suddenly afraid her confession had somehow changed the tenor of their lighthearted relationship. His intensity frightened her even as she silently prayed his feelings really were that true.

The old Ross suddenly reemerged. His eyes took on a mischievous gleam and she suspected he had hatched a plan.

"Two men," he repeated. "I think that can be arranged," he added, startling her.

"Oh?" She tried to act nonchalant, but her shaky laugh gave her away. "You have a friend hidden somewhere on the property for just such a thing, do you?"

"You're a wonderful writer, Jules, with an amazing imagination. I won't need another man for this fantasy. Only your clever mind. Go lie on the bed," he commanded, his voice deep.

"Why?" she asked, but he only shook his head and pointed to the bed. In previous engagements, when Ross took control, Julia knew to follow his commands. It appeared tonight would be one of those nights. Secretly, Julia relished being told what to do in bed. She felt herself go wet simply thinking about Ross giving her orders. Although she'd yet to disobey, she suspected she'd enjoy his punishment as much as she loved his instructions.

Rising, she walked toward the bed.

"Get undressed," he called from behind her. Turning, she

lifted her shirt in the slow, seductive manner she knew he loved. Watching his dark eyes go black with desire, she grasped the waistband of her pants, slowly sliding them off, wiggling her hips as sensuously as a belly dancer, as if she had all the time in the world. Standing beside the bed naked, she waited for his next order.

"Lie down," he said, swallowing hard as he took in her whole body. Although he'd seen her naked nearly nonstop the past week, she still adored the way his gaze ate her up as if each time was the first.

"Spread-eagle," he added, when she lay on her back on the soft bed. Following his words, she awaited his next move. "Close your eyes."

Nervous at the prospect of not being able to see him, Julia tried to lie patiently but her arousal was growing at a frenzied rate. No matter how many times he made love to her, she left each encounter frantic for more. She could hear Ross moving quietly around the room, but she was too afraid to open her eyes for fear he would stop. Whatever his game, she wanted to play it until the end.

Finally, she sensed him approach the bed and jumped slightly when she felt something silky placed over her eyes.

"A blindfold," he stated, "in case you are tempted to peek."

As he secured the scarf over her eyes, Julia instinctively lowered her arms, the idea of losing her sense of sight unnerving as well as exciting her.

He quickly grabbed her wrists and she heard a soft click. Ross had handcuffed her hands together and attached them to the headboard.

Having her bound in this manner, Ross could easily take her from the front or flip her onto her stomach according to his whims. Being blindfolded and tied up only heightened her desire for him and she had to bite her lip to stop herself begging for more.

"From this point on," he said gruffly, "you are not allowed to speak. If you do so, I will gag you as well. If you understand, nod your head."

Julia nodded, a soft moan escaping her lips. She was amazed at how easily Ross could turn her on with simply a few heated words.

The bed shifted as Ross joined her. A second later, she felt him straddle her chest, the feeling of being totally trapped and captive to his demands overwhelming and exhilarating. A soft touch to her lips was her only warning of his intentions as he said roughly, "Open your mouth." She barely had time to respond before he plunged greedily into her opening, thrusting his hard cock down her throat with such surprising need, she nearly gagged. Sensing her distress, he pulled back before pushing in again, more slowly this time.

"Suck it," he growled. "Take me deep. All the way."

Relaxing her throat muscles, Julia did as he requested. No longer a stranger to the sensation of swallowing his cock, she lost herself in the task, delighted by his groans of pleasure. Just as she sensed him reaching his climax, he pulled out. Ready to protest, she received a light tap on her cheek.

"No talking," he reminded her sternly, as she felt him leave the bed once again. He returned in only a moment and once again ordered her to open her mouth. This time, rather than tasting his musky, hard cock, she felt something cold and plastic pass her love-swollen lips.

"A ball-gag," he said, responding to her unasked question. "But for tonight, I want you to pretend it's my cock. I want you to suck it and love it just like you would me."

Uncomfortable with the obstruction in her mouth, Julia

struggled slightly against the hard toy, trying to swallow as Ross fastened the strap to hold it in place behind her head.

"Don't fight it, Brown Eyes," he said, as she attempted to reject the unfamiliar toy.

After a few minutes, Julia calmed down and accepted the bondage of her mouth. She'd given up trying to swallow and could feel a small trickle of drool escaping down her cheek.

Ross moved down her body until his legs bridged her thighs. Pushing her legs apart, he leaned forward and placed a passionate kiss on her bare mons, his tongue delving into her slippery folds to tease the hard nub beneath.

His mouth was quickly replaced by his cock and Julia groaned with relief that he didn't intend to torture her tonight. Delighted at being filled with him, she wrapped her legs around his back, silently urging him to harder, faster heights. Ross, however, did not succumb to her coercion. He leaned forward, grinding his erection into her in slow solid circles.

"How does it feel?" he whispered, his lips lightly touching her ear, his tongue tickling the rim. "How does it feel to suck a cock and have one fuck you at the same time?"

The power of his words combined with the blindfold, the toy in her mouth and his potent movements in her pussy worked their magic. She really did feel as though she were being taken by two men. A small moan escaped her throat as she tried to force him to move even faster within her.

"Not yet," he said, his breath hot and heavy in her ear. "There's still one more place to be filled."

Understanding shook her like an earthquake as he slowly pulled his rock-hard erection out of her. Her small whimpers seemed a pitiful complaint. With strong, sure hands, Ross gently turned her over on the bed before placing several pillows under her hips. With her legs still open and her upper body lowered, her ass and cunt were completely at his mercy.

His fingers returned to her clit, massaging the swollen bud until she was squirming in agony. Had she really thought this lovemaking session would be quick? She should have known better. Ross was a maestro in bed and she was his instrument. Every time he picked up the bow, he played her to perfection. Every fantasy he created was better than the last until she truly felt as though she could die from the bliss.

Panting, she tried to accelerate his movements, but he wouldn't be tempted. His fingers left her after a few more minutes and she felt him once again leave the bed only to return in an instant.

Another foreign object touched her, this time at the entrance to her pussy and again he painted a picture in her mind.

"This is a dildo, but for our purposes tonight, I want you to pretend it's me. It's my hard cock taking you. I'm going to fuck your pussy." When she moaned her pleasure, she felt his hand sharply slap her buttocks. "You aren't sucking my cock," he added harshly. Reminded of the ball-gag, she began once again to work her jaws around the toy, her mind and body anxious to please him.

Slowly, he slid the dildo inside her until it was fully lodged. Gripping the base firmly, he thrust it in place several times, perfectly mimicking his own heavenly rhythm. "That's right, Brown Eyes, fuck us," he encouraged her as he twisted the dildo, before leaving it inside her.

Satisfied with his work, he left the bed one last time. The now-recognizable coolness of the gel on her anus didn't alarm her. Instead, she delighted in its familiar feeling. As he saturated her with the lubrication, Julia could sense him applying the same to himself. His hands bumped casually into her buttocks as he rubbed the sticky gel on his cock.

Only when she felt the head of his penis at her anus did she truly cry out. "*At last*," she wanted to scream, as she realized she would finally feel that glorious, thick instrument inside her ass. Until that moment, she didn't appreciate how much she'd craved it.

The butt plug had worked its magic as Ross's hard cock entered with only the slightest amount of pain, the pleasure it produced far outweighing the small twinges at his persistent entry. Ross pushed forward without pause until he filled her completely. Every hole was filled with Ross. Every void in her life crammed full of Ross.

Moving with exquisite precision, Ross's cock plunged in her ass, propelling the dildo forward as well.

"Fuck us all," he commanded, increasing the speed and pressure of his movements. The power of all three instruments—the ball-gag, the dildo and his cock—proved her undoing. In her mind, Ross truly was three men, all of them loving her with everything they had. Her mouth worked the gag as if she were determined to give him the greatest blowjob of his life. Her pussy and ass contracted around the dildo and his cock, desperate to bring him to the same earth-shattering release that was shaking her whole body. Orgasm after orgasm ripped through her until she finally felt his own climax, his semen erupting in her ass, filling her to overflowing.

"My God," he yelled.

She felt him reach above his head as he snapped the release on the cuffs, pulled off the blindfold and unhooked the ball-gag. Below, he still remained inside her ass, seeming reluctant to leave her. Wiggling against him, she sighed contentedly.

"Spoon me," she happily whispered and he obliged,

wrapping his arms tightly around her.

"Brown Eyes," he started as she slid her hands down to her own opening.

"No," she interrupted, working the large dildo out and languidly dropping it to the floor by the bed. "Please don't leave me." Her ass deliberately clamped around him, his half-erect penis still firmly lodged in place.

"Never," he whispered. "Never."

Chapter Nine

The next day dawned bright and sunny. Ross knew immediately upon opening his eyes that he was alone in the cabin. Panicking, he gathered up his sweatpants from the chair by the fire and threw a T-shirt on over his head. Checking the bathroom, he confirmed Julia wasn't there. He headed toward the front door. Glancing out the window, he saw her shoveling snow off the path to the woodpile like a woman possessed. Frowning, he watched her for several minutes, trying to figure out what was going through her mind.

Concern ran through him as he considered his actions the previous night. Clearly, Julia was upset. She was throwing snow over her shoulder fast and furious. A two-ton plow couldn't move snow like she was. Perhaps he'd pushed her too far last night. She'd thrown him for a loop when she told him her secret fantasy. The fact that she dreamed of sleeping with two men mystified him. Of all the things he was willing to do with Julia, sharing her was not on the list. The idea of another man touching her—hell, the idea of another man simply looking at her—made him see red. He'd never be able to fulfill her fantasy in truth. Although he thought he'd certainly given it the old college try last night.

Grinning, he remembered her enthusiastic response to his lovemaking. As always, her vivid imagination allowed him to enact all of his fantasies without the fear of frightening her. Or at least, that's what he'd thought. Now, watching her cut a swath through the heavy snow, he wondered if he'd misread her responses. Had he gone too far? Pushed her too hard? He didn't think so, but her actions this morning had him perplexed. She never rose before him and as far as he could remember, he'd never seen her do anything resembling hard physical labor. Clearly she was upset about something. If not last night, then...what?

Was she beginning to feel something for him? Was his plan working? If so, then perhaps it was time to move to the next phase. He'd come too far in his plan to win her heart to turn back now, and clearly it was time to move their so-called research into relationship mode. He'd been a coward to put off approaching the subject with her this long. Once she'd worked off some of her anxiety and sorted out her thoughts, she'd come in and he would lay it all on the line. Come clean. Tell her his true feelings. Taking a deep breath, he turned to the kitchen. Maybe a nice, hot breakfast would soften her to his proposal. God, he hoped so.

℘

Sweat poured down Julia's face and into her eyes. The bitter cold temperatures and wind of the previous week had given way to a gorgeous winter day. The sun was beating down and the ski hat on her head was far too warm for her strenuous exertions. The snow weighed a ton and she could feel painful twinges beginning in her arms and back from her aggressive assault on the wet stuff.

"Why shouldn't my back and arms hurt? Everything else does," she muttered as she considered last night's fantasy for the thousandth time. When Ross offered to play out her secret sexual dream, she had no idea how much she'd pay for the request. Her jaw ached from the ball-gag and she was so sore below the waist she couldn't pinpoint where the pain was coming from. Ross had given her everything she asked for and more and even in her aching state, she couldn't find it within herself to regret a second of it. Last night had been the best night of her life and she fully expected to relive every minute of it in her fantasies for the next fifty years.

Her anxiety was not so much a result of their actions, but her feelings about those actions. She'd done the most foolish thing imaginable—she'd fallen in love with Ross Phillips. Totally and completely, head-over-heels in love. The kind of love that would never, ever die.

"How could I be such an idiot!" she repeated, the words becoming a mantra and the impetus for her forceful shoveling. Her shovel hit the woodpile hard enough to rattle every tooth in her head. "Dammit." Glancing back, she realized she'd cleared quite a wide path from the door. Unable to face the man causing her such angst yet, she turned and started to attack the driveway leading to the road.

For the entirety of her adult life, she'd avoided the overpowering, overwhelming, all-consuming feeling of love. Now in the course of a week, Ross had broken down all her well-constructed defenses and wormed his way into her heart.

"No," she whispered. Not a week. Ross had been tackling the walls around her heart for nearly a decade and she suspected he'd be most disturbed to learn that little tidbit. God, if he knew what he'd done, he'd be out here himself clearing a path to freedom as fast as his arms could shovel.

The cold, hard fact was she'd been in love with Ross Phillips since the day she met him and that love had only grown as the years passed. Every novel she'd ever written had been a tribute to him—a coward's way of expressing her feelings. She was sure he didn't realize he was the hero in all her stories. He was her knight in shining armor, her sexy, devil-may-care pirate, and her hunky, irresistible lord all rolled into one. He was the leading man in every fantasy she'd had since she turned twenty years old.

Now, she'd made the mother of all mistakes and blurred the lines between fantasy and reality. In her dreams, she was safe from inevitable heartbreak. Allowing him into her bed and her body had been foolishness at its most extreme. By keeping her imaginings private and maintaining a platonic friendship with Ross, she'd managed to hold onto him longer than any other woman in his life. The last thing Ross wanted from her, or any woman for that matter, was a permanent commitment. He was a confirmed bachelor, set in his ways. If and when he decided to settle down, it would be with a woman much more sophisticated and beautiful than her. She was the girl next door, the little sister he never had, a pizza buddy, and in just seven days, she'd thrown all that away for a brief roll in the hay. Well, maybe not brief. And certainly not a roll. More like tumbling headfirst off a cliff.

"Hell," she said aloud as she continued to make her way to the road. She was too stupid to even regret her actions. How could she feel sorry for what could quite possibly be the greatest sex ever in the history of fornication? She blushed as she recalled the image of Ross bent over her body last night as she strained to take in all of him.

Groaning, she pushed the thought away. "This isn't helping," she whispered to the trees around her. Worst of all, she had whispered the words *"please don't leave me"* to him after they'd made love. She prayed Ross had been too close to the verge of sleep to remember her foolish request. Chastising herself once again, she groaned. She'd done the one thing she never wanted to do—give him a reason to leave her. As long as the women in his bed kept things light and casual, he kept them. The moment they pressured him for more, he ran.

Even though she had known from the outset that their time in the cabin was limited, she had become used to having him in her bed. She loved eating every meal with him and telling him all of her deepest, darkest secrets. Sometimes she felt a deep connection between them that promised of a real future. He made her laugh and somehow the thought of going back to New York and their once-a-week pizza dates left a cold chill deep in the pit of her stomach.

Julia rested the shovel against a tree and lightly clasped her arms around herself—more for comfort than for warmth. She wasn't being totally honest with herself. The days in the cabin had been about more than research, at least for her. She was wearing her heart on her sleeve. Too many more days spent in his presence and the pain of his eventual desertion would tear her heart out. She had to distance herself from him now. If she was going to salvage some part of their friendship, it was time for their research to stop. One more night like last night would kill her. Even now, she felt as if her heart were bursting into a million little pieces. Better to halt things now. Imagine how much worse the pain would be later.

The day was warm and the snow was melting quickly. Once Ross realized he was no longer stuck, he'd be anxious to return to the city. Maybe he would leave today. It was still early. In fact, she'd suggest it. She could convince him she was well armed with enough research for her book.

She headed back to the cabin, resolved in her decision. Distance and time were the best things. Staring down a now-cleared road, she realized the rest of her aches and pains had disappeared. All she could feel now was the agony of her breaking heart.

℘

Ross had been more than willing to make the trek down the mountain to retrieve his SUV when she suggested it upon her return to the cabin. As he pulled up to the front porch, Julia stiffened her spine and took a deep breath. He was free. He could take his car and escape back down the mountain. Return to his life in the city. Return to his penthouse and casual one-night stands with gorgeous women. Their time was over and, although he and Julia had done enough "research" to fill a dozen books, she knew by the look in his eyes as he parked the car that he needed to leave. She would simply have to stand firm in her resolve.

"Well," he said, approaching her, "looks like Sweet Pea survived the storm just fine."

Julia grinned at Ross's continued insistence that his beloved car was a female, whom he'd nicknamed Sweet Pea. "She's sleek with smooth, firm lines that just ache to hug the road," he'd joke, running his hand across the hood. To Julia, cars were merely a way to get from here to there and all she knew about her vehicle was that it was blue and it started when she needed it to.

"Thank heaven for small mercies," Julia teased, though her heart was heavy. *It's for the best,* she silently consoled herself.

"Guess you'll be heading back to the city," she said, pleased by the strength in her voice.

"Eventually, I suppose," Ross answered, obviously surprised about her comment. "What are your plans?" he asked warily, as he climbed the stairs to stand beside her.

"I haven't finished my book yet. I'll probably stay here until it's done. If that's okay with you."

"Of course it is. I'm the one who suggested this place to begin with."

"Well," she started, clearing her throat to try and dislodge the words that were stuck there. "If you left now, you could be back in the city by early evening."

"Now?" he repeated slowly. "I wasn't really in a hurry to be on my way."

"Yes, but you aren't stuck anymore. I know you don't like to be out of the office so long. And besides," she continued before she lost her nerve, "I really need to get going on this book. It's hard to work with you constantly underfoot and even you have to admit no one's ever researched a book so thoroughly!" Forcing a light laugh, she turned back toward the cabin, anxious to escape his scrutiny.

"I didn't realize I'd been an annoyance to you," he said shortly. "You've been working steadily on the book for a week." He followed her into the house, slamming the door behind him.

Jerking at the crashing of the door, Julia twirled to face him. "Actually, I haven't even really started the book. I've just been making notes. It's too hard to concentrate with you here." She knew her tone was slightly hostile, but perhaps picking a fight would be the simplest way to get him to leave.

"Just notes?" he asked incredulously. "Pretty intense note-taking." He was obviously angry, but Julia refused to back down. Truth was that for the entire week, she'd done nothing but record every blissful moment of their lovemaking. She didn't have a plot, well-developed characters or even dialogue. Instead, all she had was a steady stream of consciousness, a mish-mash of feelings and thoughts, a disaster of an erotic diary that wouldn't sell a single copy because she would never let it see the light of day. So far, she was batting zero as an erotic writer.

Not that Ross knew that of course. He thought she'd been diligently plying her craft since her arrival in West Virginia.

"Why don't we have something to eat?" Ross said, placing his hand on the small of her back, guiding her toward the kitchen. Why wasn't he fighting with her? She was being rude and she knew it.

"I'm not hungry." She casually shrugged off his hand and crossed the room. Time to up the ante.

"Would you like some help packing?" she asked, picking up his duffel bag from the corner.

At the sight of his frown, she turned her back to him, gathering up his clothing.

"I didn't realize you were so anxious for me to leave."

"I wouldn't say anxious, Ross," she said with forced lightness, refusing to look at him. "It's just, you must admit, I haven't been getting much work done. I came here to write this book at your request."

"And I've been hindering you in that?" Ross barked. "Last I checked, I was helping you."

"With the research, yes, but let's face it, Ross, I'd say we've covered more than enough ground. I can safely say I have enough information to write the damn thing."

"Damn thing?" Ross yelled. "Well excuse me for forcing such an unwanted subject on you! I thought you wanted to write the book. I had no idea you were merely humoring me and suffering for the sake of your career!"

"Dammit, Ross. Why are you putting words into my mouth? You know perfectly well that I liked—" She paused, unsure what to call their actions. If she said making love, surely he would laugh. However, it wasn't in her to refer to their time between the sheets as merely fucking, even though that's what Ross had called it the first night they were together.

"Researching," Ross replied through gritted teeth. "That's all it was to you, wasn't it?"

Julia didn't know how to respond. Research was his word and their sexual experimentation was his idea. Surely he didn't mean for it to mean more than that. Perhaps it wasn't her casualness that was offending him. In past relationships, she'd listened as he complained about the fits of temper his jilted lovers displayed when he broke things off. Could it possibly be that the King of Casual Sex wasn't happy about her lack of emotion? What did he want? To have her clinging to his legs, begging him to stay? A watering pot? A total breakdown? Could he be that arrogant? To want some big display of dashed love? Was he angry she was beating him to the punch?

"Of course that's all it was," she answered evenly, refusing to swallow her pride and give him his show.

"Fucking research!" Ross grabbed his duffel from her hands and threw it across the room. "This is great," he yelled, fury written in every part of his body. "What have I done?"

"Ross," Julia said quietly, hoping to calm him down. "If this is about last night—"

"What about last night?" he asked.

"I know I asked you not to leave me, but Ross, you know how things are in the heat of the moment. I didn't mean it literally."

"What the hell are you saying?" He closed the distance between them until they were standing toe to toe.

Julia held her ground, refusing to take a step back even though her mind was screaming for her to retreat. Why was he so angry?

"I just wanted you to stay inside me. I didn't mean I wanted you to stay with me forever."

"I see," he said through gritted teeth, "and now you want me to leave."

Shaking his head, Ross walked to the end of the bed and sank down heavily, elbows to knees, holding his head. "Why?" he asked.

"Why?" she repeated, confused by his question.

"Why the about-face? Last night you begged me not to leave you and today you're begging me to go."

"I wouldn't say I was begging last night." Once again, she struggled to appear casual. She couldn't let him see how much his leaving would hurt.

"What's wrong, Jules? Did you make a mistake, get a little too close to the fire? Did that block of ice you call a heart start to thaw?"

His comments hit her like a punch to the stomach. "I-I don't know what you're talking about."

"Can you honestly stand there, look me in the eye and tell me you don't love me?"

"Love you?" Her hands trembled and she was uncertain what response he wanted from her. Surely he didn't want those words from her and God help her if Ross ever professed to feel love for her. She simply couldn't handle that. Love was not a forever thing for him.

"Don't be silly, Ross. You know how it is." She laughed and silently hoped it sounded lighthearted. He was far too angry and intense. She needed him to calm down. "We'd just had mind-blowing sex. Of course I didn't mean anything by it."

"Didn't mean anything by it? That's great. Just great. Talk about turnabout is fair play." Ross dragged his hands through his hair as Julia struggled to hear his next words. "Christ, the first time I give my heart and soul to a woman and she thinks it's all a fucking game."

"Heart and soul?" Julia whispered. *What the hell is he talking about?*

"After everything we've done together, shared with each other, you still don't get it, do you?"

She shook her head slowly as her knees began to tremble. Afraid they would buckle, she glanced behind her for a chair. He was the one who'd called it research. Led her to believe they were indulging in casual sex. Everything he'd done had been done to instruct her so she could write the book. Right?

"How can you not know how I feel about you?" He rose and gripped her upper arms. "Every time I look at you, I see my past, present and future. All I want in the world is wrapped up in you, Jules. I love you. Dammit, I love you and I want to spend the rest of my life with you."

Horrified, Julia broke free of his grasp. "What? What the hell are you talking about?"

Glancing around, she was amazed by how the spacious room suddenly felt stifling, as if it were shrinking. All she could feel was Ross's gaze burning into her, his words still stinging her ears. She felt hot and dizzy and perilously close to passing out.

He loved her? Yeah, right. Nervous laughter erupted from her lips before she could call it back.

"You think this is funny?" Ross whispered, his face pale, his voice strained. "I bare my heart to you and you think it's a joke?"

Julia fought to restrain the hysterical laughter bubbling up inside her. Never had she felt so afraid, so confused. Stark terror raced through her veins. She knew she should get herself under control, try to talk to him, but all that came out was uncontrollable laughter, ringing out in cackling peals until she was gasping for breath, tears streaming down her cheeks.

Oh my God. I'm having a breakdown. What if what he said was true? What if he did love her? How could she trust he would never leave her? Because that was the one thing she could never survive—losing him.

Before she could maintain her composure and try to explain, Ross turned away from her, his tone suddenly devoid of emotion. "I can see I've made a mistake. I clearly thought there was more between us and I've asked for more than you are capable of giving. Forgive me. Goodbye, Julia."

With that, he left the cabin. Julia's feet felt as if they'd been sunk into concrete. She heard the slamming of his car door and the turning over of the engine, but she couldn't move a muscle. Small gravel pelted the front door as the car sped away down the mountain and still she stood frozen in place. It felt as if hours had passed before her body gave up its fight to remain upright and she collapsed into a heap upon the floor. Great sobs ripped through her as she replayed their last conversation over and over. And the one word that continually came back to haunt her...Julia. He'd called her Julia.

Chapter Ten

The days turned into weeks and time lost all meaning as Julia worked relentlessly on her novel. She slept only a few hours a night, many times jerking awake in a cold sweat, Ross's name upon her lips. She ate when she remembered to, which wasn't very often. Twice, she ventured off the mountain to replenish her supplies. There wasn't a scale in the cabin, but by the looseness of her clothing, she suspected she'd lost at least ten pounds.

After Ross's departure, it had taken her nearly a week to pull herself from the bed and the deep depression into which she'd sunk. During that week, memories of her parents' deaths haunted her. She could swear she heard Duke meowing at various times of the day. The image of Ross's face when she laughed at his declaration of love tore her heart to pieces. Convinced she was losing her mind, Julia gave herself up to sleep to avoid the pain—only rousing to relieve herself, eat a few bites of food or throw an occasional log on the fire when the cabin became bone-chillingly cold.

After a week of self-pity, she roused herself enough to leave the sanctuary of her bed and make a plan. In spite of her best efforts not to suffer another debilitating loss, she had. Her own foolish fears had cost her the love of her life—the only man she could ever imagine marrying and having children with. Refuting

Ross's declaration hadn't saved her pain, but given it— unbearable amounts of soul-rending, heartbreaking aches that took her breath away. For two days, she plotted and planned, determined to win back the heart of her best friend. With her course set, she sat down to write. Her words were her only weapon, her only power.

In the dark of the night, when she awoke with tears streaming down her face, she sat down to write. When loneliness ate at her insides like a cancer, she sat down to write. When the memories of Ross's arms around her felt like a vise squeezing the life out of her heart, she sat down to write. Only the novel kept her going.

Once she'd roused herself from depression and risen from her bed, she started taking long walks in the snow, communing with Mother Nature as she felt the wounds of the past slowly heal. There was a lot to be said for the healing effects of the natural world.

Finally, after two months and three more snowstorms, the manuscript was complete. As a butterfly emerges from its cocoon, Julia felt she was coming alive again. Pleased with her efforts, she spent the next four days cleaning the entire cabin from top to bottom and packing up to prepare for her return to the city. The real world. Ross.

Driving down the mountain, Julia felt hopeful for the first time in weeks. Taking her time, she traveled back to New York like a lady of leisure, a person with nothing but time on her hands. Mailing her novel to Ross at the first post office she passed, she bought a map and proceeded to take every back road she could find, eschewing the busy interstates in favor of exploring the small towns along the way, even stopping in Easton, Pennsylvania to tour the Crayola Factory. Walking around the displays with a tour group of elementary-school children, she felt very much like a child herself again. It was as if she were starting her life anew, everything fresh and unique. Unfamiliar and unexplored.

She took pleasure in the small things. Trying something different to eat at a restaurant. Stopping at overlooks along the way. Watching the arrival of spring and taking in the scenery as she drove—signs of the green season were sprouting up everywhere. A city girl by birth, she'd never fully appreciated all nature had to offer until her time in the cabin.

Riding with the windows down, she inhaled the smells of budding trees, blooming flowers and rain-soaked earth. Smiling, she took delight in everything she saw, feeling as if she were a blind woman who'd suddenly been granted the gift of sight. Even her return to the city—full of hectic traffic-packed streets, cursing, angry commuters, and taxicabs blaring their horns—did nothing to dim her new, happy outlook on life. For the first time in her life, she felt free. Free to chart her course and achieve her goals. Goals she would stop at nothing to reach.

Entering her apartment exactly one week to the day she left the cabin, Julia dumped her suitcase in her bedroom and ventured out onto her tiny fire escape. Smiling, she yelled "Hello" to the familiar old neighborhood before setting out to unpack her clothing, aware her time in this apartment was waning away. Changes were coming. She wasn't the same broken girl she'd been when she crawled in and decided to call the place home ten years ago. She had money in the bank, a successful career, and options—lots of them.

Reaching over, she flicked on her radio, the sound of Gloria Gaynor belting out "I Will Survive" suddenly permeating the room. Singing along, Julia spent the entire afternoon doing all the chores she'd spent a lifetime putting off—cleaning out closets and file cabinets, putting her old life in boxes, making room for the new one.

The doorbell ringing pulled her away from her work just as the sun was setting outside and her hungry stomach was starting to grumble. A quick peek out the peephole revealed, to her surprise, Ross. Had he received her manuscript? Was that why he was here?

Taking a deep calming breath, she opened the door. She stepped back to watch him walk in with a large pizza and six-pack of beer.

"Welcome home." He passed her with barely a sideways glance on his way to the kitchen.

Stunned speechless, she watched as he put the beer in the refrigerator and grabbed a couple of plates from the counter. She silently marveled over the fact she had watched him do this very same thing a thousand times and yet even this simple act seemed different, special.

"Wh-what are you doing here?" she asked, kicking herself for the slight quiver in her voice. *Cool, Julia. Very cool.*

"It's Thursday, Jules. Pizza night," he answered as if she were two slices short of an extra large. "Got a supreme to celebrate your return."

"I know it's Thursday, but how did you know I was back?"

"I promised your landlady twenty bucks if she called me when you returned. Got the call this afternoon and settled the debt on my way up."

"My, aren't we ingenious?" She smiled tentatively, trying to determine his mood.

"I'm not without my resources." He returned her smile with a faint one of his own. "You look good."

Julia felt tears clogging her throat at his words. For once, her own words were failing her. Why couldn't she say aloud all the things she found so easy to write on paper?

He cleared a spot on the dining-room table, now cluttered with packed boxes. "Getting a jump on spring cleaning?"

"Something like that. I'm surprised to see you here. I thought after you left the cabin—"

"I made a promise to you," he said tightly.

"A promise?"

"I promised you that no matter how things ended in the cabin, we would still be friends. So here I am."

Although the words sounded friendly, the tone was forced and Julia knew she had quite a bit of making up to do to him. She'd hurt him terribly and yet her heart swelled at the knowledge he would swallow his own wounded pride to keep a promise to her. Just when she thought she couldn't love him any more, he blindsided her with kindness, when all she truly deserved was his disdain.

"Ross," she started, but he stopped her.

"I got your book," he said, his words hitting her like an exploding bomb. A small cowardly part of her had been hoping it hadn't arrived yet. After all, the novel was their story and despite the fact Ross was standing in front of her, she couldn't imagine he would want to discuss such a painful topic. Did he want to continue the fight, rehash the arguments, berate her for behaving like such a fool? Panic rising inside her, she tried to act nonchalant.

"Great," she replied, her voice tight.

"It was good," he added casually. "Really good. But, Brown Eyes—" He looked down at her. When had he gotten so close to her and had he really just called her Brown Eyes? "—you forgot to mail me the last chapter."

"Oh." She fought the impulse to step away from him. Taking another calming breath, she stiffened her spine.

"Actually, I haven't written the last chapter."

Clearly confused, Ross merely looked at her for a moment. "You never send me an unfinished manuscript."

"Well, the thing is," she kept on, praying she wasn't blushing like a fool, "I didn't like the original ending."

"Original ending?"

"It was terrible," she added hastily. "I tried it out, researched it, but it didn't really work."

"Is that right?" His voice was flat, emotionless. How she wished she could tell what he was thinking.

"In fact, I was hoping you could help me," she continued.

"Help you?" His voice betrayed nothing to her and she was tempted to shake him, slap him, anything to get some sort of reaction from him.

"Write another one." Again his face looked as if it were carved from granite. "After all, we were working on this project together."

"Help you how?"

"I have another idea for the ending." Her voice sounded strained even to her own ears. She was desperate to say the words her heart was screaming. "But I thought maybe we should research it first."

"Research." He repeated the word with such disgust, she considered running away. What if he rejected her and the new ending? What if it was too late to make amends?

"Yes," she replied quickly before she lost her nerve, "I have part of it scripted out right here." She handed him a sheet of paper from one of the numerous stacks on the dining-room table.

Glancing at the paper, Ross visibly blanched. "What the hell is this? Didn't we try this before? What are you hoping for here, Jules? Another opportunity to kick me in the teeth?"

"No. Of course not, Ross." A lone tear trickled down her cheek. "I don't want to hurt you again. Ever again. Trust me. Please."

Ross flinched as she tossed his own words from the cabin back at him. He'd asked for her trust and she'd given it—well, up to a point. Now she was asking for the same.

"Julia," he started, but stopped as an anguished sob escaped her lips.

"Don't call me that," she whispered.

"What?" he asked.

"Julia," she repeated. "Please don't call me that."

Whatever strength had gotten Ross to her apartment and through her front door seemed to slowly seep out of him as he dropped into the chair behind him.

"I don't know what you want," he said miserably.

"Just read the paper. Please." She was well aware of the pleading tone in her voice, but she didn't care. All she wanted was to finish what he'd started in the cabin, the right way this time. He was silent for so long, she knew she'd lost. He would never forgive her.

"How can you not know how I feel about you?" he started, his voice flat. Startled, she glanced up to see him reading the words on the page she'd handed him.

"Every time I look at you, I see my past, present and future. All I want in the world is wrapped up in you. I love you, Jules. Dammit, I love you and I want to spend the rest of my life with you." Crumpling the paper as the last words fell from his lips, Ross stared woodenly at the floor. He'd risked his heart for her again. Her courageous, handsome hero had given her his heart again. Only this time, she knew what to do with it.

She knelt before him. The tears she'd tried valiantly to hold in began to fall freely. This time she would answer with the words written in her heart.

"Ross," she said, her voice trembling beneath the tears. "Oh God, Ross, I love you too. More than I can ever tell you. These past couple of months have been hell. I love you so much it hurts and I'm so very sorry. Please forgive me. I never meant to hurt you and I know I don't deserve it but I swear if you'll only forgive—"

No more words came as Ross's lips descended on hers in a kiss that took her breath away. Julia clung to him as the kiss continued for minutes, maybe hours, both of them trying to prove their love with their lips, their hands.

When they finally parted, Ross laughed as Julia continued to cry—happy tears this time. Helping her to her feet, Ross crossed the room to grab a box of tissues.

"Blow," he ordered, wiping her dripping nose.

Following his command, she reached up on tiptoe to place a soft kiss on his cheek. "Please say you forgive me."

"Jules, there's nothing to forgive. I wasn't totally honest in that cabin. I hid my feelings, hoping I could trick you into falling in love with me, rather than simply telling you the truth right from the beginning."

"When did you realize you loved me?"

"Years ago." His face broke into a self-deprecating grin. "Talk about your world-class fools. So much wasted time."

"Well," Julia answered smugly, "if you've taught me anything in the last few months, it's that anticipation only makes the reward greater."

Bending down, Ross wrapped her tightly in his arms before picking her up and slowly swinging her around. Julia giggled at his impetuous action.

"I love you," he said again, spinning her faster, "and you are the greatest reward any man could ever receive."

"Ross, you lunatic," she cried, dizzy and giddy, "put me down."

Placing her back on her feet, he added to her lightheadedness with a kiss that sucked all the breath from her body. His hands loosely framed her face as he worshipped her lips with his. If she lived to be a hundred, this was the kiss she would remember on her deathbed.

"That was a pretty good ending." For the first time since he walked into her apartment, Julia saw a true glimpse of the real Ross.

"Just pretty good?" she asked.

"Not bad. It works for me."

"I'm so glad you approve of this one," she answered.

"Still..." He rubbed his chin as if deep in thought.

"Still what?" she asked, pleased by the return of his fun-loving nature.

"I don't know. The words were good, but it seems to be lacking something."

"Oh yeah? Like what?"

"Well, this is an erotic romance. Therefore I think it only fitting that after such a heartfelt declaration, the heroine should prove her love."

"Prove it how?" Julia asked suspiciously.

"Well, I'm not the writer, of course, but maybe the ending would be stronger if right after her speech, she fell on her knees and gave the hero the best blowjob of his life."

Julia burst into laughter, shaking her head. "I'm not sure a blowjob would really fit at that particular point in the plotline. Something like that is really better suited to the epilogue."

Ross groaned. "Epilogue. What is it with women writers and epilogues?"

She smiled. "What do you mean? Epilogues are extremely important to romance novels. Women like to know that things work out in the long run and that the romance doesn't end with the last chapter."

"Yeah, well. I suppose you could work the blowjob scene into the epilogue, but I'm gonna tell you right now, it better be one of those 'later that night' epilogues and not a 'five years later' one."

Julia giggled. "I'll see what I can do."

"You do that." Ross wrapped his hands in her hair to pull her close. "I'm even going to be a good editor and help you with that epilogue. Like I always say, you can never do too much research."

Epilogue One

Later that night...

Julia gave Ross the best blowjob of his life.

Epilogue Two

Five years later...

Ross watched his very pregnant wife put the finishing touches to her ninth erotic romance as their new cat, Duchess, rubbed against her swollen ankles. Since publishing her first novel in that genre, she'd become known in the industry as the Queen of Erotica, a title he took great delight in teasing her about. And, of course being such a good editor, he still helped her with all of her research.

Tequila Truth

Dedication

For Jack and Glen

Prologue

"What is your ultimate sex fantasy?" Heath filled the shot glasses with Jose Cuervo.

Colt grinned while Kylie groaned. "Christ. Surely we've answered that one before?" She knew they hadn't, but this particular question made her uncomfortable. Quite frankly, she didn't think her two testosterone-laden buddies were ready to hear about her fantasies. They believed her desires to be somewhat chaste. Silly men.

The trio had been following this same tradition since the early days of their friendship. Kylie initiated the celebration, calling it Tequila Truth, explaining that birthdays should be a time of reflection. The concept of the game was simple. The birthday boy—or girl in her case—posed a question and then each member drank a shot of tequila and answered. The only rule was the answer had to be completely honest.

Unfortunately, her attempt to bring deep introspection to her male roommates fell quite a bit short of the mark. They'd played the game since their freshman year of college and Heath's questions always revolved around sex.

"Nope." Heath began reciting past questions while ticking them off on his fingers. "Past questions have included your dream bed partner, strangest place you ever had sex and lost-virginity stories, but no sexual fantasies. I was saving this one up special." He gave her a naughty grin that let her know he wasn't fooled by her reluctance to share. By now, both men knew her well enough to know if she was holding back or wasn't being completely honest.

"For heaven's sake, Heath, why don't you try to play this game with some semblance of maturity? After all, you are twenty-five this year."

"That's an easy one." Colt licked the salt off his hand, downed the tequila and sucked the lime. Licking his lips, he settled in for a long story. He was nothing if not an imaginative storyteller. "I've got this busty blonde all to myself on a desert island. We're stranded and she's completely at my mercy. Begging me to save her and all that crap. She's wearing nothing but a bikini top and thong, as all of her clothes were ripped off during the shipwreck."

Kylie interrupted at this point. "Holy hell, Colt. Why do these imaginary women of yours always have to be blonde *and* stupid?"

Heath and Colt laughed, but she merely raised her eyebrow, waiting for his response.

Colt stopped laughing when she failed to join in. "Oh, that was a serious question? I thought it was one of those rhetorical ones."

She grinned despite herself. Colt was the ultimate male chauvinist pig and, for some inexplicable reason, she adored him anyway. He and Heath were the best friends she'd ever had and she didn't doubt both of them would lay down their lives for her. They'd mistaken her for a male—Kyle, not Kylie—when she wrote expressing a desire to share an apartment with them during their first year of college.

To soften the blow of their mistake, she'd pulled out a bottle of tequila her first night in residence. Her older brother had given it to her as a going-away present, unbeknownst to their parents. As it was her eighteenth birthday, she started the Tequila Truth game thinking it would be a great way for them to get to know one another. Several drunken hours later, the three of them were as thick as thieves and had never lived apart since.

"So what are you doing to this blonde with questionable intellect?" Heath, as always, was relishing Colt's detailed descriptions.

"Well, I don't know if you know this about me or not, but I'm a man who likes to be in control."

She gasped, as if amazed, and laid her hand on her heart. "No, absolutely not. I will *never* believe that of you."

He grinned at her sarcasm and continued. "There's some rope that's washed up from the shipwreck and this chick is hot for me. I mean way hot. She starts begging me to take her."

At this point in his story Kylie faked a bored yawn, but he continued anyway. "I grab the rope and take her over to a coconut tree. I throw the rope over one of the low-lying branches and tie her hands above her head."

"Have you ever seen a coconut tree?" she asked. "The branches are miles off the ground."

"Shit, it doesn't matter what kind of tree. Kylie, will you let me finish?"

"Fine," she answered shortly, pressing her thighs together. The problem with his fantasy was she knew exactly where it was going and she would be hard-pressed to hide her reaction. The idea of being tied up and left completely at a man's mercy was certainly pretty high on her list of fantasies as well. Definitely in the top five.

"So I tie her to the tree with her hands above her head. She's helpless that way and her whole body is mine to explore

131

and possess. I pull the thong down her legs and throw it into the sea. I tell her on this island, she'll always be naked, that she will never hide her body from me. I can tell she likes the way I'm talking to her, all stern and powerful and shit, because she starts squirming and whimpering."

Kylie struggled to stop reacting in completely the same way.

"I tell her to open her legs and she does. When I touch her, the woman is dripping wet and hotter than hell. I nearly come in my pants right there because I want her so bad. I reach into the back pocket of my ripped-up shorts and pull out a knife."

He paused briefly and looked at her. No doubt he expected her to make some smartass comment about the convenience of having a knife, but she was struggling to catch her breath, overwhelmed by her own arousal.

Colt, satisfied with her silence, continued talking. "I use the knife to cut off her bikini top and I have to step away because I'm telling you this girl is stacked, with a capital S. She's got these enormous big brown nipples and they are pointing straight at me."

He continued describing the woman's body in detail until finally she cried, "Enough. I think we get the picture."

"I'm not sure I do," Heath joked and she sent him a nasty look. "Maybe visuals would help. I've got some dirty magazines in my closet leftover from high school days. We could find a model who fits your description."

"Can I help it if I'm a breast man?" Colt asked the question with a look of injured innocence that fooled her not one bit.

"That's a rhetorical question, right?" she asked and then lifted her hand in a gesture that said *continue.*

"Well, I was going to go in to detail about how I suck the life out of those babies, but I can skip ahead. You get the picture."

"Hell yeah, I do. This fantasy is a thing of beauty." Heath sighed with appreciation apparently enjoying Colt's answer to his question.

"So once we're both good and hot, I take off my shorts and tell her to wrap her legs around my waist. She's holding on to the rope around her wrists and this woman is strong. She uses her toned legs and arms to fuck the hell out of my cock while she's hanging there naked from the tree. She's driving her cunt down on me hard and it's all I can do to hold on to her hips."

She swallowed hard as she imagined the woman riding him. Problem was the blonde wasn't a blonde, but a redhead who looked suspiciously like her.

Heath adjusted his pants under the table without bothering to hide his arousal. If there was one thing she had gotten used to in seven years of living with these men, it was that they were always functioning at half-mast. Shit, a strong breeze could arouse her roommates—she never ceased to be amazed by their intense sexuality. Over the years, she'd watched the revolving door of women who passed in and out of their lives and she'd heard enough moaning and banging headboards through the walls to last her a lifetime.

She consoled herself with the thought that through it all, she was the one constant woman in Colt and Heath's lives. Through college graduation and first jobs, broken hearts and promotions, she was the steady one, the reliable one, their buddy with boobs.

"That was hot, Colt, but not as hot as mine." Heath poured another round of shots.

"So hit us with your best shot." Colt picked up his tequila, clearly enjoying his pun and ready to continue with the drinking part of the celebration.

Heath drank his tequila shot and leaned forward. "In my

fantasy, I've got this smokin' hot babe spread across my lap and I'm spanking her full, firm ass. It's flushed red with my handprint and she's moving into my smacks while her arousal is dripping down her legs. She's begging me for more and I'm giving it to her. Then she starts pleading for my hard cock. When I think she's been punished enough, I push her down to the floor and tell her get on her hands and knees. Then I fuck her from behind, hard and fast. She's so hot she's burning the flesh off me, but I don't care. I keep pounding into her tight cunt, while she's crying and screaming for more."

She sat motionless after his fantasy for several moments before she realized her mouth was gaping and she closed it.

Colt shook his head in obvious disgust. "That's the problem with you, Heath. No foreplay. That was the worst description of a fantasy I've ever heard. You don't build the scene or give good descriptions. You just go straight to the climax, so to speak." When he finished chuckling about his second pun, he pushed her shot glass closer to her. "So what about you, little darlin'?"

Taking a deep breath, she licked the salt, swallowed the burning alcohol and skipped the lime. Before she could think about it, she heard her unspoken dream falling out of her mouth.

"In my ultimate sex fantasy, two guys are taking me the way you both described...at the same time."

Chapter One

Six months later

"Darlin', I'm going out," Colt yelled and Kylie came out of her bedroom in time to see him pulling on his leather jacket.

"Okay. Staking out again?" She finished putting in her earring as she walked down the hallway to say goodbye.

"Yep, bastard drug dealer." He was dog-tired from too many nights hoping to catch his elusive criminal. He'd served on the police force since his graduation from college with a degree in criminal justice. He'd made detective last year and was often undercover. Much as he grumbled about the hours, he wouldn't trade his job for anything.

"You'll get him this time, Detective." Kylie gave him an encouraging smile.

He wolf-whistled with appreciation as he glanced at her loose hair, silky shirt and tight jeans. "Well, look at you, hot stuff. Got another date with the mystery man?" He tried to appear uninterested though it gnawed on his nerves that she wouldn't tell him anything about her new beau. Hell, she wouldn't even give him the man's name. Not even Heath could sweet talk it out of her and she told him damn near everything.

Kylie claimed she was sick of him doing background checks on all of her dates, then combining forces with Heath to scare the men off when they decided they weren't good enough for her.

She didn't have to deal with the scum of the earth day after day like he did. If she'd seen a quarter of the ass-wipes he'd put behind bars during his time on the force, she'd thank them for their diligence. Thing was, none of her past boyfriends had lasted as long as this guy, and he tried not to think about it, as the fact was driving him slowly insane. She was his roommate and one of his best friends. He'd never screw that up for a roll in the hay and truth be told, he'd never really seen her as a woman he might seriously pursue until Heath's birthday party nearly six months ago. Since then, he'd become obsessed with the thought that her ultimate sexual fantasy was to be tied up and spanked by not one lover, but two. It had been easy to keep his hands off of her as long as he'd believed she was a vanilla girl in his rainbow sherbet world.

"Be careful." She leaned forward and placed a chaste kiss on his cheek and he fought the urge to turn at the last minute to capture her sweet mouth with his own. He'd never given her more than a friendly peck, but lately he found himself consumed with the sight of her luscious pink lips and all the things he'd like those lips to do to him.

"I'll probably be out all night. You okay here...alone?" Heath was out of town doing work for his architectural firm and wasn't expected back for another week.

She laughed away his obvious, not-so-clever attempt at discovering whether or not she would be sleeping by herself. "I'm a big girl now and as hard as this may be for you and Heath to grasp, I can take care of myself."

"Yeah well, just make sure Romeo drops you off at the door. We're out of coffee. Besides, it's a school night and you have work tomorrow." Kylie was a social studies teacher at the local high school and he imagined the teenage boys must line up to get into her class. She was petite and sweet in a sexy kind of way.

"Colt Hardin, you ass. I'll have you know I can invite any man back to my room that I want. God knows I've listened to enough of your sleepovers."

He frowned at her words. He hadn't invited any woman back to their place in years and he was annoyed at her for dragging up ancient history. Hell, a man couldn't be held accountable for inconsiderate actions committed during his drunken college days forever. Unfortunately, his cell phone rang before he could take her to task.

"Hardin. Yeah, I hear you. I'm on my way." He snapped his phone shut. "I gotta go. Just be careful, eh?"

She looked at him with suspiciously cute innocence and he felt the effects all the way to his gut. "Oh I will."

As he left the house, he tried to kick back the instinct that told him she wasn't going to be careful at all. Not...at...all.

When Colt pulled into the driveway, it was not long after midnight. At least he hadn't been stuck on an all-night stakeout. In fact, he'd gotten damn lucky as his not-so-bright drug lord actually struck an illegal deal right under his nose within thirty minutes of his arrival. He'd filed all the paperwork, dotted all his i's, crossed all his t's, and was looking forward to at least eight hours of uninterrupted sleep.

As he walked down the hallway to his room, he heard an unfamiliar sound coming from Kylie's room. He was surprised to find her home already and a bit annoyed at the prospect of hearing her with some lover. Continuing past his own room, he stopped outside her closed door. Again the strange, sharp sound came, but this time it was followed by Kylie's cry of pain.

"Please stop," he heard her whimper.

He tried the doorknob only to find it locked. Impatient to get inside, he leaned back and kicked. The doorframe splintered and the door fell in.

It only took him a second to take in the horrifying scene. Kylie was naked and tied facedown on her bed. Her wrists were secured to the headboard, while her ankles were bound together at the bottom. A man Colt had never seen was standing over her, striking her with a belt. Her ass was covered with painful-looking welts and she was crying for the man to stop.

At Colt's entrance the man froze mid-strike, but Kylie, obviously in pain, continued to thrash against her bonds in an attempt to escape.

"What the fuck is going on here?" Colt bellowed. She flinched at his voice and her struggles became even more earnest.

Without thought to his actions, he crossed the room in three steps and led with a right hook that had the man on the ground with one blow. Bending down, Colt picked the man up by his shirt only to beat him down again. The man threw his arms over his head protesting, but he was too enraged, too furious to hear anything but the pounding of his own blood in his ears. Finally, one sound made its way through to his consciousness.

"Colt!" Kylie cried. "Colt, please stop. Please. Stop!"

The man was cowering on the ground and Colt struggled to catch his breath. Turning slowly, he saw her fighting desperately to break free. "Untie me. Please." Tears were streaming down her face and he felt his anger rise again at the red-hot swelling on her ass and legs. "Untie me," she repeated and Colt quickly crossed to the bed to release her.

As soon as she was loose, she scrambled under the blanket, obviously anxious to cover her nakedness. She winced the second her rear-end hit the bed and his hands clinched into fists again.

"Stop, Colt. Please. Don't hit him anymore."

At her request, the man on the floor seemed to rouse himself. "Who the fuck is this guy?" He bellowed the question at Kylie who looked down at her hands, clutching the blanket tightly around herself and avoiding his gaze.

"He's my roommate." Her voice was trembling slightly and Colt fought to get a deep breath.

"Roommate!" The man hissed at her.

Colt turned slowly to face the man, more than ready to resume the pummeling, but she must have sensed his intent.

"No." She grabbed roughly at his arm before he could swing again. "Colt, no."

He looked down at the jerk on the floor. "You're under arrest."

The man stumbled to his feet, wiping blood away from his mouth. When he looked at Colt, his face was snarled with rage. "For what?"

"Assault and battery. Attempted rape."

"Colt," Kylie cried as the man laughed humorlessly.

"You can't arrest me for any of that. She asked me to do it. She asked for it all."

He drew back his arm to strike again, but she held tight. "Colt, I mean it. Stop now." Her voice was stronger and it caused him to turn around. "What Scott said is true. Just let him go. I'm not pressing charges."

"Kylie?" His heart felt lodged in his throat as he took in her tear-stained face.

"Let him go," she repeated and Scott's cold laugh assaulted his ears again.

"Told you so. She likes it rough. Don't you, sweetheart?"

He turned so quickly Scott never saw it coming. Colt's fist connected with his jaw and laid the man out yet again.

"Jesus Christ," Scott shouted. "I'm the one who's going to file for assault, you fucking asshole."

"Get out." The words came from between his clinched teeth and his fury was barely contained. The man must have sensed the danger as he gathered up his belt, jacket, and shoes and ran out of the room without another word.

She dragged in a shaky breath as she leaned back against the headboard and he watched tears form in her eyes.

"What the fuck just happened here?" He struggled to contain the rage that was clogging his chest.

She refused to meet his gaze or answer his question, so he repeated it as he dropped down to sit next to her on the bed. When she failed to answer a second time, he placed his hand on her chin and lifted her face until she had no choice but to look into his eyes.

"I'm not going to ask you again, darlin'."

"It was a misunderstanding. Everything is fine now. Really. You look beat, Colt. Why don't you go on to your room?"

"Are you crazy? Did you bump your head? I'm not going to bed until I get some goddamn answers."

"Nothing happened here." At his angry look, she seemed to rethink her words. "I mean, I think things just got a bit out of hand."

"That man had you tied up and was beating the hell out of you, Kylie. I'd say things were more than a bit out of hand."

"It was a mistake, that's all."

"He said you asked for that beating, but I happen to know for a fact, my best friend has more intelligence than that."

She bit her lip and a tear escaped her lovely brown eyes before she could swipe it away.

"Aw hell, darlin', please don't cry. I'm right here and I won't let that man touch you again, I swear it. I'm just trying to understand—"

"I did ask him for it."

He studied her face for a moment, sure he'd heard her wrong.

"Look at me," he demanded.

When she complied, he repeated her words in his question. "You asked him to beat the hell out of you?"

"No," she cried, "of course not. We...we were starting to get intimate. He seemed like a decent man—" Colt snorted at her words, but she continued anyway. "I mean we've been going out for a few months and I thought I could trust him. He asked me what I liked...I mean in bed, and I told him—"

She stopped talking and tried to look away.

"You told him what?" He refused to let her escape and held tight to her chin, forcing her gaze to meet his.

"I told him I've always wanted to be tied up and spanked." Her words were no more than a whisper, but they resonated in his head like a cannon.

"You didn't like what he was doing, Kylie. Regardless of what you asked for, I've got eyes in my head and I know he was hurting you."

She shuddered and closed her eyes tightly before responding. "You're right," she conceded. "I hated what he was doing. It hurt, but he wouldn't stop, no matter how many times I asked him."

"Then why the fuck didn't you let me arrest the bastard?"

"Because I asked him to tie me up. Christ, can you see me sitting in front of one of your friends down at the precinct stating my case? I asked him to do that to me."

Her tears fell freely now and his heart froze at the sight. He'd never seen her cry. Not in all their years together as roommates. She was a tomboy, to be sure, and was most at home in a room full of itching, cussing, drinking men. She watched football and hockey with the same rabid enthusiasm as him and her language would make a sailor blush. She owned one dress that he'd ever seen and she'd only worn that for a funeral. She'd never had a manicure and she cut her own hair, usually in a snit when it finally drove her so crazy she had no choice.

"Kylie, why?"

At his question, he watched her tears evaporate and the same tough exterior he'd grown used to reappear.

"I'm tired, Colt. I think I'm going to go to sleep."

"Kylie—" He started to repeat his question, but she cut him off.

"Don't. Don't ask me. Please, leave me alone."

He considered her request as he studied her face. He knew her well enough to know she wouldn't say anything more on the subject. Not tonight, not tomorrow, probably not ever.

"Roll over." His words were harsh, but he wanted her to understand she could deny him the truth, but she would not deny him this.

"What?"

"You don't want to talk—fine. You want to be left alone—fine. But I'm not leaving this room, darlin', until I've seen for myself, with my own two eyes, that you aren't seriously hurt.

Now we can do this the easy way or we can do it the hard way. Roll over."

The seriousness of his expression must have convinced her refusal was futile. She smiled slightly and tried to cajole him out of his anger. "You're just trying to sneak a peek at my ass."

When her half-hearted joke failed to produce a response, she sighed heavily and rolled over. The blanket covered her and he had to reach up to pull it down. When he did, it took all the strength in his body not to chase down her so-called boyfriend and kick the shit out of him again.

"It doesn't hurt." Her words were muffled by the pillow, but he could read the lie inside them.

He reached out slowly as if to touch her, but Kylie must have read his intent as she flinched away quickly, pulling the blanket back up. "I'm fine. Good night, Colt."

He narrowed his eyes at her dismissal, but rose to leave.

"I'll fix your door tomorrow, darlin'."

She didn't answer, so he didn't say anything more. Besides, he had some thinking to do and a phone call to make. It was nearly one a.m. and Heath would cuss him out for waking him up, but he didn't give a shit. The time for action had come and serious changes were on the horizon for Miss Kylie Halston.

Chapter Two

It was early Friday afternoon when Heath let himself into the house and dumped his suitcase by the door. Colt was obviously waiting for him and hollered from the living room.

"I'm in here."

Heath walked into the room to find Colt sitting on the couch with his feet propped up on the coffee table, nursing a beer.

"Bit early to be drinking, don't you think?"

Colt gestured to a second bottle near his feet. "Brought one out for you. It should still be cold."

Heath smiled as he grabbed the bottle and dropped down into the recliner. He loosened his tie and took a deep breath. "Damn, it's good to be home. I hate hotels and airports."

When Colt failed to respond, Heath looked around. "Kylie still at work?"

"Yep. She should be back in a couple of hours." Colt took a swig from the bottle. "Gives us time to decide how to deal with her."

Heath started scraping at the wrapper on the bottle. He was still in shock over his friend's phone call four nights earlier. Colt's recitation of Kylie's date from hell made his blood run cold.

"I've been thinking about it for days and I've decided it was that fucking Tequila Truth question of yours that started this mess." Colt pulled his feet down to the floor and leaned forward. "That damn sex fantasy question. I've watched Kylie flirting with dangerous situations more and more these last few months and I know it's all because of the seeds we planted. Hell, you had to pull her out of that sex club over the summer."

Heath nodded. "As hard as she kicked me, I'm surprised she didn't leave me with a permanent limp. She didn't appreciate getting yanked out of there like a naughty teenager."

"I don't give a shit whether she appreciated it or not. You were right to do it. She could have been hurt in a place like that." Colt ran a hand through his shaggy brown hair, a sure sign he was frustrated and pissed. "She's not being careful. She's messing around with things she doesn't know anything about."

"You're right about the game exacerbating the problem, but you're not going to heap all the blame for this at my damn door. This is our fault—together." Heath stressed the word *our*. "We've always treated her like another one of the guys, never holding back our locker room talk. It's no wonder she's interested in doing a little experimenting. The way we go into fucking detail about every climax."

"Thing is, Heath, we haven't done that in months. Not since your twenty-fifth birthday party."

He and Colt had been shaken to the core by Kylie's sex fantasy, both imagining themselves in starring roles. Ever since then, they'd shied away from sharing their bedroom escapades and Heath wasn't sure he could explain why. He felt, at least from his point of view, he was being unfaithful to Kylie somehow, which was utterly ridiculous considering he'd made no promises to her.

Mari Carr

Heath leaned his head back and sighed heavily. "Well, maybe it's up to us to give her what she wants." He studied Colt's face closely as he spoke, trying to gauge his friend's reaction. He didn't think Colt would be opposed to the idea and even suspected his friend had been considering the same thing. Since Colt's phone call, he'd certainly had plenty of time to think about the two of them taking Kylie to bed and fulfilling all of her sex fantasies. "Think about it, Colt. One weekend with no-holds-barred where we give Kylie everything her little heart desires."

Colt leaned back in his chair and as the minutes dragged on, Heath worried that perhaps Colt's mind hadn't been wandering in the same direction after all. His worries proved unfounded with Colt's next words.

"Well, I'll tell you right now, if she agrees, I intend to get a promise out of her that she'll let us meet all of her boyfriends in the future on the first damn date."

"That's a good idea." Heath was relieved by Colt's agreement. However, he was less confident about securing Kylie's. "You think she'll go for it?"

"Think about it, man. Kylie is stubborn as hell when it comes to getting what she wants and in this case, she wants to explore her sexuality. Problem is she doesn't know how to go about it so she keeps trying all these damn stupid, dangerous things. She's dating assholes simply because she thinks they'll be more amenable to playing kinky bed games. She went to that damn sex club—alone, for God's sake. She's too innocent to see she's going about it all wrong. What would have happened to her if I hadn't come home early the other night?"

Heath repressed a shudder at the thought that had been haunting him since Colt's phone call. One of the things he loved best about Kylie was the unabashed, enthusiastic way she approached life. She held back nothing. What you saw was what you got with Kylie Halston. She lived with two men regardless of what society might say about it, simply because she preferred the company of men. If she saw something she wanted, she went after it because, as she was fond of saying, she didn't intend to have any regrets at the end of her life.

"There is one thing that's been bothering me, Colt. One thing that almost stopped me suggesting this whole idea. We've never shared a woman. I don't give a damn how experienced we are, we've always operated solo. We could hurt her even worse than that prick from the other night."

Colt grinned as if he'd expected this argument. "We won't hurt her, Heath. I'd rather cut off my left nut than hurt that girl and I know without a doubt you feel the same way. She's our girl. She has been since the day we met her. Besides, buddy, you are the only man in the world I'd share a woman with."

Heath considered his words. Damn cop was right. Kylie was their girl and if he'd ever been tempted by the prospect of a ménage, Colt and Kylie were the only people he trusted enough to try it with.

He and Colt had been best friends since elementary school and Colt knew him better than his own mother did. Then Kylie drifted into their lives the year they all turned eighteen and something had clicked.

Nevertheless, he still wasn't sure he should have initiated this conversation, regardless of Colt's enthusiasm for the idea. His true concern had very little to do with sex and more to do with Kylie's response. "She'll resist us. Turn us down flat."

"At first maybe, until she realizes what we're offering her."

"We've skirted around the sex thing with her in the past, Colt, and she always says the same thing. She's not about to ruin friendship for sex."

Mari Carr

"Number one, we haven't teased her about sex since the early days and number two, we all knew back then none of us were serious about it. It was playful talk after one too many beers. This time we're serious and she'll see that."

"So how do you want to play it?" The more they talked about it, the more anxious Heath was to begin. The prospect of being able to take Kylie to bed was creating a serious tightness in his suit pants.

"We're not going to play it at all." Heath was confused by his words until Colt explained. "I think it's time we let our natural impulses come out."

Heath groaned. "Shit, we'll scare the hell out of her."

"Heath, think about it, man. We're talking about all the fantasies we can squeeze into a weekend. She'll know if we're holding back. We'll simply lay out the plan and let nature take its course."

"We both lean heavily toward the Dom side, Colt. You don't think that will present a big problem? Kylie's way too independent to take orders from us lightly."

"That's just it. I'm not sure she wouldn't love to be dominated in bed."

"You think Kylie is a sub? How many beers did you drink before I got here?"

Colt shrugged. "It's just a feeling I have. Besides, don't forget, she wants to be tied up and spanked, not the other way around. She'll love every command we give her. Dammit, it was your idea. Are you going to do this or not?"

Heath stood up and walked back toward the front door and his luggage. "Of course I am."

"Good. Go unpack and then we'll plan how to proceed."

"Actually," Heath confessed, "I did a little shopping while I was away. Come back to my room and I'll show you all the stuff I bought for our weekend party."

"Kylie won't know what hit her." Colt grinned.

Heath shook his head and held up his hand before Colt could state the obvious. "Yeah, yeah, yeah, I got the damn pun."

Chapter Three

Turning off the car, Kylie sat in the driveway and studied her house. She was surprised to find it flooded with light. She knew Colt had the weekend off and she expected him to be getting ready in his bedroom to go out on some hot date with the newest member of the Bimbo of the Month club. Heath wasn't due back for a few more days, so she anticipated having the house to herself. She certainly needed the time to evaluate where she was going so wrong in her life. The episode with Scott still haunted her and she hadn't had a decent night's sleep since then. That, added to the fact the bruises on her ass were only beginning to fade, kept her irritable and on edge.

Her damn roommates had ruined her. All their talk about sex and bondage and toys and spankings and, oh hell, she felt like she'd spent the last seven years in a fog of sexual frustration. She wasn't an innocent by any stretch of the imagination. Despite her lack of girly-girl genes, she dated fairly regularly, although she couldn't recall having a real boyfriend since high school. Ever since she moved in with Heath and Colt, the men who drifted in and out of her life—and sometimes her bed—couldn't compete. Her roommates were the yardstick by which she measured every man and sadly, every single one came up lacking.

She beat her head back against the headrest and closed

her eyes. She'd love to rail at the two men causing her all this angst, but neither one of them had a clue how much they affected her. To make matters worse, the cocky bastards would have a field day with it if she told them. Teasing was second nature to all three of them and she could imagine the fun they would have at her expense with such knowledge. Despite all her sarcastic comments about their cavemen attitudes, she desperately wanted them. Both of them. That was the other problem. When she thought about sex with her roommates, both of them were present. Sure, some her fantasies involved one or the other, but always there was the knowledge that both of them were with her.

"Yeah," she sighed. "Like that will happen." She had no one to blame for her lonely state except herself. She'd rebuffed their flirting at the beginning, demanding to be treated like another guy and, as luck would have it, her demands were met tenfold for seven long years.

The front door swung open and she watched Colt step out on to the front porch.

"You gonna sit in that damn car all night?"

She grinned at his gruff manners. Colt was a true cowboy, born and raised on a ranch outside of Dallas. He moved with a slow, country grace that never failed to take her breath away.

Climbing out of the car, she laughed as she walked toward him. "Waiting for me?" She couldn't help but be pleased at the idea, no matter how unlikely.

"You're late." His voice was rough and she got the sense he was angry for some reason.

"I decided to get my grading and planning for next week finished at school, so I wouldn't have to drag it home. Now I have the weekend all to myself. Are you going out tonight?"

"Nope. I'm in for the evening. Don't you have a phone in

that classroom of yours? You should have called. I was starting to get worried."

Kylie felt a tremor of confusion at his words. Although they typically called if they were held up, there was no hard and fast rule about checking in. "Sorry, Colt. I figured you'd be going out for the night. I didn't think it mattered when I got home."

"It matters," he grumbled.

As soon as she walked in the house, Heath emerged from the kitchen with his hands on his hips.

"Well, it's about damn time. Where the hell have you been?"

"Welcome home to you too," she teased as she walked over to give him a friendly kiss on the cheek. "We didn't expect you back until Tuesday."

She was shocked when Heath turned at the last second and her welcome home kiss missed his freshly-shaved jaw and landed straight on his lips. She tried to jerk back, but two strong arms wrapped around her and held her in place as he deepened the kiss before finally releasing her.

The entire embrace couldn't have lasted more than a few seconds, but she staggered back when it ended as if she'd drunk a whole bottle of wine.

"Now that's worth coming home to."

Kylie shook off his actions and words, thinking perhaps it was her roommates who'd been drinking. She caught the light scent of beer on Heath's breath.

"Start the party without me?" she asked.

"Nope. We were waiting for you." Heath winked at her and returned to the kitchen. She stood for a moment trying to understand the unfamiliar tension she felt in the air, but before she could sort out her thoughts, she felt Colt's strong arm encircle her waist. He pulled her back against his chest and his breath tickled the hair on the back on her neck.

"Colt?"

"You hungry, darlin'? We were about to throw some steaks on the grill." At his words, he moved her into the kitchen with his arm wrapped tightly around her.

She glanced over her shoulder, uneasy with his casual closeness. Heath smiled at them as they walked in and acted like there wasn't a thing in the world wrong with the way Colt was holding her.

"I picked up some T-bones on my way home from work. Hope you're hungry."

She was completely flummoxed. "Are we celebrating something?"

"The weekend," Colt replied, releasing her with a quick kiss on her cheek. He crossed over to the refrigerator to pull out a bottle of her favorite wine. When he reached for three wine glasses, instead of one, she narrowed her eyes. Colt and Heath never drank wine—ever. They were strictly hard liquor or beer men.

"Okay, that's it. What the hell is going on here?" She placed her hands on her hips and struggled to stop her toe from tapping in annoyance. Her mother was an angry toe-tapper and Kylie had, much to her chagrin, picked up the habit. To add to her aggravation, both men merely laughed at her pose and continued about their duties as if she hadn't spoken at all.

Once Colt had the wine poured, he carried a glass over to her.

"Watch your mouth, darlin'. Ladies shouldn't cuss."

"Lucky for me I'm not a fucking lady. Now what the hell are you all up to?"

Colt shook his head at her response, putting her wine glass

down on the kitchen table. Then he even had the nerve to *tsk* at her. "I'm afraid that filthy mouth of yours is going to get you in a whole heap of trouble. What do you think, Heath?"

She watched Heath's expression flicker between amusement and anger before he turned his smoldering gaze toward her. "I think it's a shame that ass of hers is too sore for what I've got in mind. You're looking to get punished, Red, but after that stunt you pulled the other night, you no doubt need more time to heal. Best not push us too far."

She felt her face flush with embarrassment and fury. She whirled on Colt. "You told him?"

"'Course I did, darlin'."

"It was none of his business. Shit, it wasn't any of yours. This is unbelievable." She felt betrayed and mortified and completely out of her element.

"None of my business?" She flinched at Colt's heated reply. "Is that what you just said? Let me tell you something, Kylie Halston, you made it my business when you brought that son of a bitch into our house and let him abuse you. You listen to me now and you listen good. Your willful, impulsive, reckless days are at an end."

"What's that supposed to mean?" She was taken aback by the anger in Colt's face. Never in all their years of friendship had he lost his temper with her and she didn't doubt she'd tested him plenty. Out of the corner of her eye she saw Heath coming toward her and was shocked to see the same intense look in his gaze.

"It means," Colt said, stepping closer, "that from this point on, you answer to us."

She burst into laughter at his haughty reply. "Ha!" she yelled before common sense kicked in. Neither man seemed pleased by her dismissal.

Heath reached out and ran the back of his knuckles down her cheek. She gasped at how much the simple touch affected her. "Ah, Kylie. It would seem you need a bit of convincing."

"Can you two please stop talking in code? I haven't understood a word you've said since I got home. It's like I've dropped into the Twilight Zone."

Heath's hand stopped caressing her face and ventured around the nape of her neck where his grip tightened and he pulled her closer to him. "You want plain-speaking? Fine. The terms of our friendship are on hold. For the rest of this weekend, you aren't simply our roommate or our buddy. You're going to become our lover as well. From this moment on, you're ours."

Speech seemed to desert her. One word kept resonating in her brain. The only word she seemed able to process amidst the rest.

"Ours?"

Heath grinned as he repeated the word. "Ours." Then he bent down and kissed her.

Chapter Four

Colt watched Heath kiss Kylie as if his life depended on it, and he couldn't help but recognize the same sense of desperation in himself. Her resistance to Heath's kiss only lasted a second and Colt grinned as her hands slowly began to creep up his friend's chest and around his neck. He'd never studied a kiss this close up—at least not one he wasn't participating in. He was struggling with the impact it was having on his libido. Damn, it was making him hot.

Sensing the kiss was coming to an end, he reached over and pulled her toward him. "That looked pretty good. Give me a taste."

She never missed a beat and offered him the same luscious response she'd given Heath. Their girl was nothing if not resilient. Most women would be screaming the walls down if they'd been pounced on like this, but instead, here was Kylie clinging to him and playing tongue tag as if they'd been intimate for years.

As he pulled away, he placed a playful kiss on her nose and watched her blush in response.

She took two steps back and he started to follow, but she threw up her hands to ward him off.

"Oh no—no more of that until I get some answers."

Colt nodded. "Good point. We have a few things we need to

get straight before we get down to the fun stuff."

She stiffened slightly at his words, but he simply took her hand and tugged her toward the kitchen table, helping her into a chair.

"Drink your wine." He pushed the glass at her and she all but gulped it down.

"Not so fast," Heath admonished. "You're not going to get drunk."

"Given the way you two are acting, I'm thinking drunk would be an excellent state for me tonight."

Colt fought against the chuckle growing in his chest. God, she was a spunky little thing.

Heath, however, didn't seem to be amused. "I mean it, Kylie. That stunt you pulled the other night was damn stupid."

"We are *not* discussing that subject." She stood up as if to leave, but Colt rose first and pushed her back down.

"Well, darlin', I beg to differ on that point. In fact, that episode the other night seems to be one in a long line of asinine actions on your part. As of right now, those games are over."

"I don't know what you're talking about."

Heath reached across the table and took her hands in his. Colt continued to stand behind her chair with his hands on her shoulders. There was no way she would escape until they laid out their scheme and did that little extra convincing Heath mentioned, if necessary.

"If you wanted to try some kinky sex, Red, all you had to do was ask us."

"What?" Kylie squeaked.

Colt bent forward until his mouth was next to her ear. "You're sick of missionary style and you want to do some experimenting. There's nothing wrong with that."

He felt her shudder at his words and from his bird's eye view caught sight of her hard nipples poking through her T-shirt. Oh yeah, she was listening.

"Problem is you're going about it all wrong. You need to experiment with men you can trust."

"And you and Heath are those men?"

"Oh yeah," he whispered in her ear.

Heath leaned closer and Colt knew the action was deliberate. They were boxing her in so she could get used to being surrounded by their large, hard bodies. "One weekend, Kylie. This weekend. Every sexual fantasy our imaginations can cook up."

"And then? What happens Monday?"

Colt wasn't surprised by the question. Her main concern regarding sexual involvement with them had always revolved around preserving their friendship.

"Monday, life returns to normal," Heath explained, but Colt wasn't entirely satisfied with that answer.

"Except," he added, "you have to agree to stop putting yourself in dangerous situations. No more sex clubs or assholes. We expect that promise from you, Kylie. It's the one point of this deal that is non-negotiable."

"And if I promise to let you bully all my future dates, you'll agree to do anything and everything I want this weekend?"

Colt fought back a smug grin at her question. He'd had more than a few tense moments in the hours since Heath had made his proposal. Colt was terrified she would not only refuse their offer, but get so upset by it she'd move out. The woman had funny notions about how the world should work and his main fear was pushing her out of their lives altogether with this suggestion. Her question was accompanied by the "Hallelujah

Chorus" in his head as he felt certain she was about to agree to their terms.

Heath grinned up at him. "Oh, I think 'anything and everything' is definitely negotiable. Don't you, Colt?"

"Hell yeah."

Kylie reiterated the terms once again and Colt knew she needed the reassurance. "So let me get this straight. You two are offering me one weekend of sexual fantasies with the promise that it won't change or ruin our friendship."

Heath leaned back in his chair and crossed his arms across his chest. "I think that about sums it up."

Colt watched as she pondered their proposal before smiling. "Fine then. I accept your offer."

"Well," Heath said, "I think we're going to need a quick game of Tequila Truth."

"Why?" Kylie seemed surprised by his request. "It's nobody's birthday."

"I have a burning question I need answered and only absolute honesty will do." Heath rose quickly to grab the bottle of tequila out of a cabinet.

Colt seemed nonplussed by the impulsive game and grabbed the salt and shot glasses before opening the refrigerator. "No limes."

"We'll have to do without." Heath sat down and started pouring the liquor.

"I'm guessing this question, like all of your others, will follow suit and deal with sex?" She was teasing him and Heath smiled. He and Colt were definitely about to drag her out of her comfort zone and yet she still managed to retain her sense of humor and fun. Thankfully years of friendship had built a solid foundation of trust between three of them because he was certain that without it this suggestion would never succeed.

"Wouldn't want to break the streak. Okay, what fantasy do you want to have fulfilled this weekend?"

Colt nodded approvingly and Heath mentally patted himself on the back. By discussing what they wanted to do in the game, they made sure there would be no misunderstandings. He was determined to meet her needs, but at the same time, he knew he and Colt both had their own personal agendas in regards to Miss Halston's lovely body. By talking it out first, they could gauge her reactions and minimize the risk of scaring or even possibly hurting her.

Kylie reached down and picked up her glass, draining it. "If you'd made this offer a week ago, I think my answer would have been different."

"Bondage," Colt said. "You would have asked to be tied up."

She nodded. "I'm afraid of that now."

"We'll do it. Look at me." Heath took her hands in his and waited until she raised her gaze to his. "We will never hurt you, Kylie. The point of this whole weekend is to allow you to ask for whatever you want without fear. It's us," he added with a shrug. "You know we'll take care of you. Besides, one of the mistakes you made with that idiot the other night was in not setting a safe word. Pick a word right now. Any word and if you say it during this weekend, we'll stop what we're doing right away."

"Hitler," she replied.

"What?"

"My safe word. It's Hitler."

"Well, that's disturbing." Colt was teasing, but she merely shrugged.

"We're studying World War II in my class right now. It was

the first thing that popped into my mind."

"Hitler it is." Heath leaned back and picked up his own glass. "I want to watch you give Colt a blow job while I fuck you from behind."

Her eyes grew dark and she squirmed in her chair. "Oh yeah, we could do that."

Colt seemed to agree. "Damn that sounds good. Darlin', look at me." She watched as Colt picked up his own shot glass.

He knew what his friend was going to ask for before the words left his lips. They'd discussed it earlier and it was the one thing both men wanted more than anything.

"I want to fuck your ass while Heath takes your pussy. At the same time."

Heath watched and silently said a prayer, but Kylie never blinked an eye at Colt's fantasy.

"Oh yeah," she said with a grin, "we can definitely do that."

Chapter Five

"Bedroom." Colt stood and pointed down the hallway. "My bedroom. The bed's bigger."

The trip to the other end of the house seemed to take a lifetime as none of them could resist stopping for kisses and tantalizing touches along the way. Colt had worried it would feel strange having another man so close to him as he made love to a woman, but after years of friendship, he and Heath seemed to have a sixth sense about what to do. It was exhilarating to watch Heath and Kylie kiss as he wrapped himself around her from behind, his own lips trailing down her soft neck.

When she turned around and offered her lips to him, he loved knowing Heath was watching them, loved how hot Kylie got from the things Heath was doing with hands that Colt couldn't see.

As they entered the bedroom, Colt kicked the door shut behind them and Kylie walked toward the end of the bed.

"Undress for us," he said as she turned to face them.

He watched her face go through a gamut of emotions—from embarrassment to nervousness before settling on the one he'd only seen in his dreams.

A sexy smile touched her rosy lips as she slowly pulled her shirt up and over her head. He expected to see one of the sports bras she usually wore and was shocked to discover his tomboy roommate owned a black, lacy concoction that was completely feminine and showcased more cleavage than he'd realized she possessed. He fell back against the door. How could he have missed those babies in the last seven years? Fuck, she was built like a brick house.

Not finished with her seductive torment, she released the clasp on the bra and let it fall off her arms to the floor. Then she brought her hands up slowly to cup herself and he felt his blood pressure rise to a decidedly unhealthy limit as she lifted her breasts up, taking the nipples between her fingers and squeezing. Glancing over, he saw her striptease was working its magic on Heath as well. The man was rubbing his immense erection through his jeans. Not a bad idea, he thought, and he reached down to try and relieve some of the pressure building in his own pants.

"Kylie," he whispered, spellbound by her sultry movements.

Turning slowly, she looked back over her shoulder with a grin that proved she knew exactly what she was doing to them. Kicking off her shoes, she peeled her pants and panties off together, down over her hips, one torturous inch at a time. As she bent over, he and Heath were treated to a perfect view of her luscious round ass as she slipped the material off. There were some fading bruises there and he realized they needed to take care not to hurt her.

He staggered toward her, but she skittered away until she stood beside the bed.

"Come here," he barked out, his voice betraying his need, but she just giggled at the sound.

"You two come here." She crawled up on the bed, gesturing for them to join her.

Colt began to unbutton his shirt, his eyes never leaving her lovely body, and he sensed Heath doing the same thing. Her gaze seemed to eat them alive as she watched them undress and he felt the reins of control slipping through his fingers. Damn woman was trying to top from the bottom and they were letting her. He looked over at Heath and watched the same realization enter his friend's face.

"Open your legs," Heath said sternly as he pulled his shirt from his shoulders, discarding it without a thought.

Colt saw her face flush, though whether with excitement or embarrassment, he couldn't decide. Unable to reign in his dominant desires, he reached over and roughly pulled her legs apart.

"Like this," he said. "Next time we tell you to open your legs, we want them exactly like this."

He watched Kylie's breasts rise and fall as her breathing hitched up a notch, but he was sure now her response was not based on fear, but arousal. She was responding to them like a true submissive. He felt like pumping a victory fist in the air.

Placing a bent knee on the bed, he leaned down until his mouth hovered above her gorgeous pussy. The sweet smell of honeysuckle washed over him. He looked over his shoulder and Heath gave him a quick, encouraging nod.

"Do it," his friend whispered and Colt turned back to heaven. Kylie's hands flew to his hair as he pressed his lips to her hard clit, his tongue probing and pushing. Her hips began to move against him, but he denied her movement by placing his firm hands on her upper thighs.

"Don't move," he ordered.

"Please, Colt," she begged breathlessly and he returned to torment her drenched opening with his mouth. Circling the entrance to her body with his tongue, he felt her muscles tensing and suspected his little firecracker was already perilously close to exploding.

Dipping his tongue inside her hot cavern, he only managed to thrust twice before Kylie's body shuddered violently beneath his touch and he heard her relieved cries.

He sensed Heath moving behind him and heard the unmistakable sound of pants and shoes hitting the floor.

"Move, Colt." Heath's demands were husky and harsh and he suspected his friend was hanging on by a thread. He chuckled as he pushed away from Kylie's heat.

"Poor Heath," she teased, reaching up to pull him down to her. "No foreplay, just climax."

He fought against the laughter as Kylie repeated his own words from the Tequila Truth game that had started them down this path.

Heath joined their laughter, leaning over her flushed body. "That's why I brought Colt along for the ride, Red. Now put this damn condom on me. If I'm not in your body in the next thirty seconds, you're going to see that climax up close and personal all over your stomach."

She took the condom Heath had retrieved from the stash he'd put in the nightstand. Colt had to grab one of the columns at the end of his four poster bed as she ripped the package open with her teeth and he felt the groan that passed Heath's lips in his own gut. She took sexual teasing to a whole new level.

As soon as Heath's cock was sheathed, he plunged into Kylie's body and once again, Colt was struck by the incredible pleasure he felt in watching the act. Never a fan of porn movies, he couldn't understand how the mere sight his best friends making love could impact his senses so thoroughly. The pressure in his body grew to such a rate that he raced to strip off his own jeans.

Kylie continued to arch into Heath's thrusts and Colt's last tether of patience broke. Unwilling to remain apart from the action any longer, he climbed onto the bed until his hips were even with her head.

"Yes," she hissed impatiently and he thought she seemed annoyed at his tardiness.

Heath looked up as she reached over to draw Colt's rock-hard erection in her mouth.

"Wait," Heath cried as he pulled out of her body. "Roll over, Red."

He recalled Heath's fantasy and grinned at her eagerness to comply. No sooner had she landed on her hands and knees then she was scrambling for his cock. Her hot breath caressed him as Heath resumed his place in her pussy.

Gripping her hair gently in his fists, Colt guided her mouth to him and nearly fell forward at the first touch of her tongue against the crown of his cock. She swirled around the tip, sucking off all the pre-come gathered there.

"Shit," he muttered. "Open up, darlin'. Let me in that sweet mouth of yours."

Kylie responded to his words and enveloped nearly half of him in her first pass. He was shocked by her daring response. He was by no means a small man and was accustomed to women balking at the thought of trying to take him in at all. Kylie, however, seemed frustrated at not being able to get enough. Each time she moved, she took him deeper until Colt felt the back of her throat. With rough hands on her head, he tried to pull out, afraid of choking her, but she growled—literally growled—at his attempts and he loosened his grip.

"You feel so good, Kylie. Oh, baby. I want to fuck your mouth."

Colt glanced up to see a frown cross Heath's face. No doubt his friend thought he was pushing her too hard, too fast. Kylie released his cock and looked up at him with something close to desperation in her eyes.

"God, yes. Please do it. I want both of you to fuck me hard and fast."

Colt grinned at the shocked expression on his friend's face. Apparently neither he nor Heath had been paying close enough attention to their little roommate. This wildcat had been living under the same roof with them for years and neither of them realized what they'd been missing.

"Hold on, darlin'." He pulled her mouth back down to his cock and pushed in without hesitation.

Heath resumed his place in her cunt and together they began to thrust in unison. He would bury his hard length in her throat on Heath's retreat. As Heath moved forward, he moved back. Over and over they moved as Colt struggled to slow down his building climax. He tried to distract himself by counting Kylie's orgasms, which seemed to be coming continuously now with little build up time in between. He'd reached four when he heard Heath explode. The sound of his friend coming was the last nail in his coffin and he erupted into her mouth, relishing the feeling of her swallowing down every drop of his come.

None of them spoke a word as they collapsed on the bed. Heath dragged Kylie's limp body in between them, spooning her from behind as Colt placed kiss after kiss on pretty, flushed face.

Chapter Six

Kylie awoke to the sound of whispers in the dark room, but she was too exhausted to figure out who was speaking or what they were saying. Hell, she was too tired to care where she was. A slight tug on her wrist brought the truth crashing down around her. Weekend. Fantasies. Heath and Colt.

Her eyes flew open as she felt another strange pull, this one near her ankle.

Looking around, she saw Heath at the head of the bed securing her right hand there with a silk scarf. At her feet, she watched Colt tighten the final knot that secured her, spread eagle.

"No," she whispered, starting to fight against the sensation of being helpless. Heath leaned down and kissed her gently.

"Hush, Red. We aren't going to hurt you and you have your safe word, remember?"

She nodded numbly trying to overcome the irrational fear permeating her body. Colt must have sensed her distress because he started loosening the scarf at her ankle.

"No," she cried. "Wait, please." She tried to take a deep breath, but couldn't seem to get enough air into her lungs.

"Dammit, Kylie. We don't have to do this. I'm untying you."

"No, Colt. Please. Just give me a minute."

Heath lay down beside her, surrounding her with his comforting warmth. "You don't have anything to prove."

"You don't understand," she said, struggling to still her racing heart. "I wanted this. Used to dream about it and Scott took that away from me. I was such an idiot to trust him."

Colt joined them on the bed, claiming the other side of her. It was strange, she thought, that a few silk scarves left her feeling helpless, while being surrounded by these two, huge strapping men made her feel inordinately safe.

"You're damn right you were." Colt's words were harsh and she saw Heath give him a dirty look.

"You weren't there, Heath. You didn't see what that man was doing to her. She put herself at serious risk and if I live to be a hundred, I'll never be able to erase the image of her, hurt and helpless and crying. Shit, it's the last thing I see every night before I go to sleep and it eats me up inside."

Kylie's throat seized at his confession. The words seemed to flow straight from his heart and she had never heard her old-fashioned, stoic friend ever sound so vulnerable. She'd been so wrapped up in her own self-remonstration and guilt; she never stopped to think how much her ordeal had affected him.

"I'm sorry, Colt."

He gave her a crooked grin, apparently embarrassed to have revealed so much. "That's okay, darlin'. At least I got to kick the guy's ass. Heath missed out on the brawling part. Not that I needed his help. Did you see that guy by the time I finished with him? He was blubbering like a baby."

Heath rolled his eyes and she couldn't resist adding to Colt's ribbing joke.

"You were very macho and strong." Her words evoked an annoyed groan from Heath.

"Good God. You don't need to stroke that ego."

"Unfortunately, I don't seem to be able to stroke anything at the moment." She wiggled her fingers and laughed as both men seemed to grow an extra appendage at the same time. Glancing down at their naked bodies, she added, "Ooh, look who's come out to play."

Heath thrust his rejuvenating erection into her hip as Colt leaned forward and captured one of her nipples in his mouth. She sucked in a breath as his teeth toyed with the tip, amazed by the sudden sensitivity of her breasts.

"That looks tasty," Heath murmured.

"Lucky thing I have two."

She expected Heath to laugh before realizing the joke was on her. His bright blue eyes narrowed in on her breasts and he leaned down to stake a claim on her offer. While Colt continued to tease her with his teeth and tongue, Heath's response was to use only his lips to suck on her, hard and deep. The contrasting actions were almost more than she could stand and she marveled at her coming orgasm. Christ, she'd never come from someone fondling her breasts and yet she couldn't deny the pressure building below.

"Oh God," she screamed as her body splintered with the sheer pleasure of it. "Holy hell." She trembled and struggled against her bonds, not from fear, but frustration. She needed someone hard inside her—now.

The sound of soft laughter and Colt's "slow down" alerted her to the fact she'd made her demand out loud. Sadly, their response didn't soothe her ragged nerves.

"Now," she repeated, through gritted teeth. "One of you needs to get inside me now."

Heath's smile hovered, but a flash of annoyance seemed to cross Colt's face and his dark eyes narrowed.

"Darlin', you've got to learn that you don't go around making demands here."

"Who says?" Her voice was confrontational, but she didn't care. She was barely clinging to her sanity.

"I say and Heath says. In case you failed to notice, you are tied up, Kylie." His frown was replaced with a wicked smile. "At our mercy. Ours to torment and take whenever we feel like it."

She pressed her hip against Colt's hard-on and gave him a sultry grin when he hissed. "Feels like you'd like to now."

Heath laughed at their sexy banter and she turned her heated gaze toward him. Of the two men, she suspected Heath would be the most susceptible to her demands.

She lowered her voice, adding a huskiness she hoped he wouldn't be able to refuse. "Heath, I need you. Put your big cock inside me, baby, and fuck me. Please."

Heath's laughter died and his eyes seemed to darken.

"Geez, she's good," he muttered.

"And naughty as hell." Colt leaned up and turned her face back to his with a strong hand on her jaw. "You're playing with fire, darlin', and believe me, the only one who's going to get burned is you. Now behave yourself and you'll get everything you're asking for."

She started to protest, but Heath must have decided to save her from herself as he bent down and claimed her lips in a kiss that screamed passion and possession. His tongue forced her mouth open and swooped in to tangle with hers. The power of the kiss was overwhelming by itself, but intensified when she felt Colt's fingers drifting softly along her stomach.

Her hips rose in an attempt to capture Colt's touch, but every time he seemed on the verge of giving her what she most desired, his fingers detoured, stroking the tops of her thighs, her knees, her hips. She wanted to scream at him, rant and rave and insist that he touch her where it would do the most good, but Heath wasn't giving her a chance to complain. His tongue and teeth were tormenting her lips and she was struggling to breathe from the onslaught of his kisses.

Finally, she felt one of Colt's callused fingers against her clit. Just a quick tap and it was gone, but the touch was enough and she fought against the bonds at her feet, desperate to rub her legs together for some sort of relief. She heard a strangled cry and realized it was coming from her. Heath responded to the sound by releasing her lips.

"I think our girl wants something a bit stronger, Colt."

Colt didn't respond with words, but with another tap, this one harder, on her clit. She bucked up into his touch, but his hands continued to elude her.

Heath's lips trailed along her cheek until he reached her ear. Pulling the plump lobe into his mouth, he nipped lightly at it, his warm breath teasing her as much as Colt's hit-and-run fingers.

"Please," she whimpered.

"Oh yeah, Red," Heath whispered in her ear, his voice darkly seductive. "I like the sound of that. Beg us. Beg us to fuck you."

Kylie's independent streak wanted to fight against his dominant demand, but that seemed to be the only part of her body not willing to acquiesce. The rest of her was pleading...big time.

In the meantime, Colt's touches were becoming more frequent, harder, longer and the power of speech deserted her entirely.

Heath continued to whisper in her ear. His words wrapped themselves around her and turned her on as much as Colt's fingers. Colt's strokes grew bolder as he alternated between the teasing taps on her clit and his circling rubs around her wet opening. He gathered up her juices rubbing them into her labia. She wanted to ask him to put his fingers inside her, but realized the men were determined to move at their own pace and they'd only prolong the torture if she fought against their control.

"We bought a toy for you, Kylie." Heath's hushed words traveled on a mere breath. She sensed Colt reaching for something, but didn't complain as he continued to caress her.

"It will get you ready to take both of us into your body." Heath continued to explain as Colt reached down and released the scarves securing her ankles to the bed.

"As you've seen for yourself, Colt and I aren't exactly small men and your pussy alone is as tight as it is sweet."

She was gasping for air, the potent power of Heath's words combining with Colt's nonstop actions, paralyzing her to everything but the coming of her own climax. Colt briefly rubbed the spot around her ankles where the scarves held her before lifting her legs over his shoulders. She could feel his hot breath near her pussy and tried to use her legs to draw him down to her. He chuckled darkly at her attempts. She couldn't budge the man. Instead of giving her his mouth, his fingers returned and she flinched as he unexpectedly drove two of them deep into her vagina.

"Yes," she hissed.

Heath's hands drifted down to toy with her breasts, but his touches there were light and gentle, a direct contrast to the hard way Colt was fucking her with his hand. Heath continued to whisper in her ear.

"Have you ever been fucked in the ass?"

She shook her head, thrilled by the intimate question. At

Heath's words, Colt's fingers left her, drifting slowly back to that forbidden portal. His fingers were dripping with her arousal as he pushed one digit into her completely.

He groaned and she could sense the impact that sound had on Heath.

"Do you like that, Red?" he asked.

She nodded her head jerkily as Colt pulled out to the fingernail, then shoved back in again. Her ass was on fire and her mind was struggling to absorb the impact of the feeling. That was only one finger. What would it feel like to have Colt's cock inside her there? Heath wasn't lying. Both men were well-endowed, thick and heavy.

"I can see you're worried, Kylie." Heath's fingers never stopped their gentle ministrations to her breasts and she marveled that she could feel them there despite the overwhelming stimulation of Colt stretching her ass.

"We won't hurt you and believe me, before this weekend is over, you'll be begging both of us to take you there. Now breathe."

Colt's finger left her ass entirely as she released the breath she didn't realize she'd been holding. His hand ventured back to her gushing pussy and gathered up more moisture. When he returned to her ass, this time it was two fingers tunneling into her.

"God," she gasped, but he continued as if she hadn't uttered a sound.

"Feels tight, doesn't it?" Kylie wasn't sure how Heath was so in tune with Colt's actions, as his head never lifted from the pillow, his lips never left her ear. "It'll get tighter, just wait. We bought a butt plug for you."

Colt's two fingers were fully enclosed and she fought back a scream as he opened them up inside, scissoring them around

174

her virgin flesh.

"The plug's not as large as we are, but it will get you ready. We're going to put it in you tonight and then Colt's going to get his turn inside that gorgeous pussy of yours."

She moaned at the picture Heath was painting with his heated words. "Yes, please."

"Then you're going to sleep with the plug inside you, filling you, stretching you."

Her hips buckled up off the bed and she struggled to grasp the orgasm that was hovering right outside her reach. Colt's muttered curse fell over her and she gave him back one of her own when he withdrew his hands from her completely. He didn't want her coming yet.

Heath bit her earlobe in warning. "Now, now, Kylie. No bad language. If there's only one thing I regret about this weekend, it's the fact that I can't spank that gorgeous ass of yours. We may have to negotiate for another night after you've healed so we can work that fantasy in."

She shuddered at the suggestion, desperate for the reality of it.

"She's close, Heath."

Kylie flinched at Colt's deep voice. He'd been silent through the entire episode.

"Are you ready, Red?" Heath never moved, his lips and hands still soft and soothing against her overheated skin.

"God yes," she said. "Please."

Something cold touched her ass and she squirmed with surprise.

"Colt's putting some lube in your ass. It'll make it easier for him to push the plug inside."

No sooner had Heath spoken than Colt matched his words

with the action. Something hard pressed against her nether hole and she started to protest its size.

"It's bigger than his fingers, Kylie, but not as big as us. Don't fight it. Let Colt slide it in, baby."

She fought to release the tension gripping her. She wanted this. She wanted it so badly she could taste it and with that thought, she felt her muscles give way. The toy slid in to the hilt, leaving her full to bursting.

Before she could think about the reality of it, she heard Colt opening up a condom and her hips lifted of their own volition. A whole rainbow of colors began to swirl behind her eyes as she felt her climax coming to claim her. The toy in her ass, Heath's soft kisses and whispered words, and the mere thought of Colt's hard cock were enough to push her over the edge.

Colt's words brought her back from the precipice once again.

"Don't you dare come until I get inside you, darlin', or bruised ass be damned, I'll spank you."

"Then hurry your ass up!" The words flew from her lips and she felt Heath's laughter against her neck.

She expected Colt to be angry and was surprised by the humor lacing his voice as he replied, "Yes ma'am," and plunged into her in one thrust.

Chapter Seven

Kylie's orgasm gripped his cock on the first shove and the tight clamping of her pussy muscles almost drove him over the cliff. Colt gritted his teeth against the impulse to give in to it until his jaw ached with the effort. Heath would never let him live it down if he came so quickly and for the first time, he considered why sharing a woman with his best friend might not be so great. If he'd been alone with Kylie in the bed, he would have given in to the orgasm, apologized, then fucked her again when he got himself together.

Right now, it was all he could do to hang on. Kylie's pussy was so hot and wet and with the plug lodged in her ass, she was tighter than a virgin. Colt wasn't sure he'd ever really grasped the words *heaven on earth* until that moment. Christ, she was a wet dream come to life. Between her moans and Heath's erotic words, it had been all he could do to get the condom on. He'd never been harder or hornier in his life and watching as Heath kissed her through her orgasm was not helping his resolve to hold on.

Closing his eyes, he forced several deep cleansing breaths into his lungs as he tried to think of anything except the tightening of his balls. Puppies, his mother, the Queen of England, anything to distract him—then she moved against him and everything else fell away. He retreated almost halfway before his body rebelled against his mind and pushed him back in. Over and over, his internal war was waged in a series of shallow thrusts until she cast the fatal blow. Her body trembled with yet another orgasm and this time, he was helpless to defend himself.

"Fuck," he cried, his climax almost painful in its intensity. Come spurted from the end of his cock in such abundance he wondered if the condom could hold it all.

"Beautiful," he heard Heath mutter as he fell to the empty side of the bed, sucking in air in great bellows that reminded him of a thoroughbred horse after a race.

He felt Kylie's small hand lying lifeless on his chest and wondered when Heath had untied her. Reaching up, he drew it into his own big paw and dragged it up to his lips where he kissed it.

Heath repeated his earlier sentiment and he looked over to see his friend grinning at their exhausted forms.

"I've never seen a woman in the throes of an orgasm. I'm usually too busy trying to keep my eyes from rolling back in my head to appreciate the beauty of it. I could watch Kylie come a thousand times and never get sick of it."

"I think I did come a thousand times." Kylie's eyes were tightly closed and her voice was hoarse. Her teasing words, so like her, lightened his heart. Heath's original concern about giving her all of themselves melted away like butter in the sun. She was with them in this adventure—hook, line and sinker. More than that, she was every bit their equal. Her obvious enjoyment of their bed play, undeniable trust and lusty nature proved once again that Kylie Halston fit them to a tee, and while that thought thrilled him to his toes, it left him slightly uneasy as well. When this weekend was over, how on earth would they ever return to their platonic friendship?

As he glanced at Heath, he saw the same concern written on his face. They listened as Kylie's breathing grew slower and deeper as sleep claimed her. When they were sure she was asleep, Colt started to voice his fear.

"No." Heath cut off his question with a quiet whisper. "It's too soon for regrets. There will be plenty of time to figure this out at the end of the weekend. Let's not worry about it until then." Then Heath gave him a cat-who-ate-the-canary grin. "I have no intention of spoiling one second of this."

Colt glanced down at Kylie's sleeping form. "Me either," he acknowledged. Then before he could stop the words, he added, "She's incredible, absolutely amazing."

"More than amazing," Heath agreed. "Better get some rest, buddy. Something tells me we're going to need our strength."

Heath woke up alone in Colt's bed. He frowned when he heard his friend's off-key singing coming from the shower in the bathroom next door. Damn them.

He hopped out of the bed and stomped across the room, annoyed that Kylie and Colt had failed to wake him and were leaving him out of their water play. He was about to slam the bathroom door open when the sound of dishes rattling in the kitchen drew him up short. Colt was clearly showering alone.

Shaking himself for his anger, Heath headed down the hallway, grabbing a pair of sweats from his room and pulling them on before heading toward the smell of breakfast.

Kylie, dressed in his T-shirt and nothing else, was standing by the stove, frying up last night's dinner. Heath rubbed his empty stomach as it dawned on him they'd forgotten to eat it.

"Now there's a tasty-looking breakfast."

Kylie threw a grin over her shoulder that changed immediately to a frown when she noticed him looking at her and not the food.

Pointing down at his apparent erection, she said, "Put that on the back burner, Frank Jr. I'm starving to death and nobody's getting any more sex until I eat."

Heath laughed as she called him by the nickname she'd given him in college. An architect, he idolized Frank Lloyd Wright the way most teens idolize rock stars. Upon graduation, she dubbed him Frank Jr. and started calling Colt Baretta. The nicknames didn't really stick and only reemerged whenever Kylie was annoyed with them.

"Seems to me, Colt and I worked pretty hard at keeping you filled up last night." He walked toward her as he teased.

"Back off, buddy. I have a spatula and I'm not afraid to use it."

He laughed and gave her a playful swat on the ass. At her sharp intake of breath, he looked down.

"The plug," he said, the hunger in his stomach forgotten. "You still have it in?"

Kylie flushed slightly and he marveled at the sight. The woman never blushed.

"You didn't say I could take it out," she answered quietly.

"Show me." His words were a demand as he was desperate to see the sight he'd missed last night.

"W-what?"

Stepping back, he pulled out a kitchen chair, sat down, and gestured for her to come closer. "Bend over and show it to me. You forget—Colt had the seat with a view last night. Not me."

"But—"

"I'm not asking, Kylie."

She licked her lips and he watched her brown eyes go black with arousal. Oh yeah, she was certainly more than a little bit submissive. He wondered how in the hell he'd missed that part of her personality for so long. Then he considered her actions with him and Colt. She was a tough-talking tomboy. She'd never shown her feminine side to either of them. No wonder she was running around like a loose wire, all that electricity and passion locked up inside her body, looking for a place to escape.

As soon as she was within arm's reach, he grabbed her hips and turned her away from him.

"You better not have panties on under that shirt, Red."

Even from behind her, he could see her tremble at his words. Slowly, she leaned forward and her borrowed T-shirt crept up her hips, revealing her to him fully.

"Grab your ankles and don't move," he demanded. He intended to soak up every bit of her bare offering. He drank in the sight of the plug lodged firmly between her butt cheeks. It was shiny from the juices slipping out of her pussy and he wondered if she stayed wet or if her arousal had started flowing when he joined her in the kitchen.

Drawing his eyes away from her stretched anus, he saw for the first time the bruises that were fading along the back of her thighs and ass. Reaching out slowly, he dragged his fingertips across the injured flesh.

"I should have been here," he whispered and once again, he felt the unbelievable guilt that swamped him whenever he thought about the abuse she'd suffered at Scott's hands. While he was grateful Colt had been here to help her, he couldn't dismiss the thought that he should have protected her somehow.

She shuddered at his touch and started to rise. He wanted

to chastise her for moving without his command, but his words were lodged in his throat.

"It was my fault." She turned to face him and her hands reached down to caress his face. He grabbed her hands and started kissing each fingertip. "I was stupid and reckless. I made a bad judgment call and I meant what I said last night. You and Colt aren't to blame."

"Why didn't you come to us, Kylie?"

Kylie laughed and then gasped as he sucked one of her fingers into his mouth suggestively. "I had no idea you guys would be so accommodating. We're friends, Heath. Friends don't ask friends to tie them up and spank them into an orgasm."

"Says who?" Colt's deep voice came from the doorway. Heath released her hands and stood up quickly, expecting to see the same anger he'd felt upon waking and thinking he'd been left out. Instead, he saw desire etched in the lines of his friend's face and it hit him. When he thought Colt and Kylie were showering together, his anger hadn't been based on jealousy, but instead on disappointment at being left out. Fact was, he would have no problem with Kylie and Colt alone together if he wasn't around, and from the look in Colt's eyes, Heath saw his friend felt the same way. He tried to process the importance of that revelation. He and Colt were truly sharing Kylie. Jealousy and petty one-upmanship would never enter into this relationship.

Kylie shook her head at Colt's comment and returned to the stove. "I'm going to tell you what I just finished telling Frank Jr. Nobody's touching me until I eat."

"Frank Jr., eh? Well, looks like somebody woke up on the wrong side of the bed." Colt's joke affirmed he knew their little wildcat was irritable. "Somebody must be hungry."

"Ungrateful girl doesn't appreciate our efforts at filling her up last night. Or this morning."

Colt's gaze narrowed and zoomed to her ass as he said the last.

"Tell me you're still wearing that plug, darlin'."

"I'm wearing it, but one of you is going to have to take it out soon. Nature is calling."

Heath laughed. Only Kylie would be so bold and honest.

"Later," Colt growled along with his own empty stomach. "Right now, I want some of that breakfast. Steak and eggs. My favorite."

Chapter Eight

After stuffing themselves on a hearty breakfast, Kylie stood up and stretched. "I need a shower. Desperately."

"A shower sounds good," Heath replied, wiggling his eyebrows at her.

"Oh yeah, I'm in," Colt added, taking the dirty plates to the kitchen sink.

"You just had a shower." She was trying to determine how all three of them would fit in her tiny shower stall.

"Well now, darlin'. There's a difference between a cleaning shower and a recreational shower."

"I was planning on taking a cleaning shower."

"And I'm going to take a recreational one while helping you get clean, so it works out perfectly."

"We won't all fit in my shower."

"That's why we're using mine." Heath grasped her hand tightly in his and started pulling her toward his room.

About two years ago, it had dawned on them they were wasting their money on rent while waiting for their lives to become more settled. None of them were in a long-term relationship and they realized it was foolish to continue flushing their hard-earned money down the drain while waiting for some life-altering change to come along. After a long discussion, they decided to invest in property and buy a house. The verbal agreement was that when one of them wanted out, the other two could buy out that person's share or they'd simply sell and split the profit.

The second they'd seen this house, they knew it was tailor-made for them. It was in a safe suburb with a reasonable commute time for all of them. It was a nice-sized ranch-style home and the layout allowed Heath to tinker with the floor plan, increasing the room sizes and adding a bathroom to his and Colt's rooms. Kylie had settled for the master bedroom because it met her needs perfectly as is. Her bathroom, though small, had all the essentials and although Heath offered time and time again to expand it, Kylie refused the offer. A bigger bathroom meant more to clean.

Heath, an architectural genius as far as Kylie was concerned, had created a bathroom oasis in his own room. A large stained glass window filled nearly one whole wall above the Jacuzzi tub, allowing in copious amounts of light while assuring privacy. In addition to the tub, he'd installed a double-headed shower stall that was nearly as big as the bathroom itself. Colt and Kylie teased him mercilessly for his extravagance, but Heath insisted he was an adult who worked hard for his money and if he wanted a big bathroom, then by God, he was going to have it.

She had to admit hindsight was 20/20 and no doubt, she and Colt would be eating crow by the end of this water party.

Colt must have felt her pain. "I don't suppose you're going to let us take this shower without adding an 'I told you so' to the end."

"Oh, hell no. You two had a lot of fun at my expense when I built that bathroom. I'm not sure I'll be able to wait 'til the end to rub it in." Heath stroked his hands together in expectation of having the last word.

"Well, I certainly hope you don't wait until the end to rub it in. I may not be able to last that long." She ran her hands over her breasts, massaging them deeply to make sure Heath caught the proper meaning of her words.

Heath groaned at the image, but Colt merely laughed before bending down and throwing a squealing Kylie over his shoulder. "Bathroom, now."

No sooner had they reached the room than Colt had her T-shirt over her head and discarded on the floor. He and Heath quickly stripped out of their sweats, standing before her in all their naked glory.

"Mmm. As I recall, you agreed to do anything and everything I asked, isn't that right?"

Colt narrowed his eyes at her question, obviously seeing the flaw in their earlier promise. "Anything with you. I'm not touching Heath."

She laughed at his comment. "Why on earth would I want your hands on Heath when they could be touching me? Although, now that I think about it, the idea of the two of you—"

"Forget it," Heath barked as he turned on the water.

"What did you have in mind, darlin'?"

"I want to give both of you a blow job...at the same time."

Colt seemed to consider her request, realizing the close proximity he and Heath would have to maintain for that to happen. "That seems do-able. What do you think, Heath?"

"Hell yeah. Come here, Red. Let's get that toy out of you first."

She gasped at the feeling of Heath sliding the butt plug out of her oh-so-slowly and shuddered at the sudden emptiness.

Fortunately, she didn't have long to miss it. Colt followed her into the shower and, using some shower gel from the shelf, reached around her to work the lather into her breasts. Over and over, he rubbed the bubbles around her hard nipples, coating them with the masculine-smelling soap. It was Heath's scent that tantalized her, birchwood and lemon balm.

Heath directed one of the showerheads at her and his hands joined Colt's in rinsing the soap off her. As the suds trailed down her belly, Heath gathered some up and rubbed them into her pussy. He scrubbed the hair covering her mons.

"I'd love to shave this hair off you," he murmured against her lips as he kissed her.

"God, yes." Colt seemed to share Heath's desire. "Think about it, darlin', nothing between you and our lips."

"Our fingers," Heath added.

"Our cocks." Colt dragged his hands down from her breasts and lightly rubbed her belly.

"Do it," she whispered, entranced by their words, hands and lips which seemed to be setting her on fire everywhere. The water suddenly seemed too hot for her scalded skin and she started to ask Heath to cool it off. Before she could make the request, Colt's arms enveloped her whole upper body, arms and all in a tight embrace. She felt something sharp at her pussy and looked down, shocked to see Heath on his knees before her with a razor in his hands.

"Hold still." Colt issued the warning in her ear and the two of them watched in silence as Heath carefully shaved her.

"That looks so hot, darlin'." Colt released her when Heath finished and rose and both men dragged their fingers over the too-sensitive flesh.

"Oh my God," she cried, pleasure crashing through her. "That feels so good."

Colt chuckled and turned her head to face him, kissing her hard and long. She was amazed by the sheer power in the kiss. Both Heath and Colt were masters and she wondered how she would ever be able to settle for the lukewarm kisses of other men after the scorching possession with which these two men had marked her with their lips.

She forced Colt to release her, remembering her earlier request. Both of them had offered her so much this weekend and she was anxious to give something back.

She slowly drifted down their bodies, pulling her hands along their chests until she reached her knees. Heath, sensing her direction, changed the flow of water from the showerheads so that it hit both men on their lower hips. She smiled at his ingenuity. It kept the water out of her face, but managed to provide plenty of moisture for her to use her hand on one man while sucking on the other.

"Kylie." Colt's voice rumbled over her and his hands were rough in her hair. She reveled in the feeling. He was always so in control that it humbled her to know she could do this to him. Leave him so hot and needy he forgot everything except what she was doing to him.

Her tongue darted around the hard head of his penis and she savored the pre-come coating him there. Turning slightly she repeated the action on Heath and wondered at the difference. She never realized a man's come had its own distinctive taste until that moment. Colt's was salty, like seawater, while Heath's had an almost nutty flavor.

Gripping each man's cock in her fists, she gave in to the desire to consume them. While she deep-throated Colt, she worked her hand hard against Heath's turgid flesh. Then she switched. Over and over, she worked her tongue, teeth and hands over their erections, acutely aware when the tenor of their play progressed to the final stage. Heath's grip on her shoulder became almost painful as his climax approached. Colt's hands engulfed her scalp, forcing her further and further down on him.

"I'm coming, Red," Heath cried when she took him to the back of her throat. He pushed her away from him. "I want to spill on you."

Colt groaned at his words and placed his large fist over hers, pumping it hard and fast against his thick flesh before releasing her. "Together. Lean back, darlin', and hold up those gorgeous tits. Let us paint them."

She quickly moved into the position he requested, swamped by the passion raging within her. The idea of being marked in such a way was potent. Pushing her breasts up with one hand, she reached down to fondle herself. She was only a second away from coming herself. As she played with her clit, she looked up at Heath and Colt, watching her as they pumped at their own erections. None of them was going to make it much longer. No sooner had the thought passed her mind then she cried out, her orgasm drenching her hand. Colt and Heath reacted to the sound as if they'd been scorched by a flame and they emptied themselves on her chest at the same time with harsh cries.

Reaching up, she ran her hands through their sperm. With a saucy grin, she looked at Heath. "What was that you said earlier about rubbing it in?"

Chapter Nine

Colt rolled over and looked at the clock, marveling at how time ceased to matter. They'd stayed awake nearly all of Friday night, not bothering to rise until lunchtime on Saturday. After an afternoon spent showering, dozing and fucking, they'd fallen asleep. Now it was three a.m. on Sunday morning and he realized they'd failed to eat dinner again.

Rubbing his empty stomach, Colt looked over at his best friends sleeping peacefully beside him. Kylie was draped over Heath with her leg hiked up around his waist, her hand on his chest, and her head on his shoulder. He grinned at the image they made, both sprawled out and disheveled.

I could wake up like this every day of my life.

As soon as the notion crossed his mind, he attempted to push it away. Too many times this weekend, he'd found his thoughts drifting to *what if?*

Punching his pillow, he tried to find a comfortable position for sleep. Unfortunately his mind continued to race with the question that kept haunting him.

What if they made this arrangement permanent?

Who said they couldn't change the rules of the game? After all, it was their game. What if they snubbed their noses at conventional society and accepted the fact that the three of them fit? They were perfect together. The words had been on

190

the tip of his tongue several times, but he'd never seemed able to voice them aloud to his friends. Something always held him back.

What if Kylie agreed, but Heath didn't? Or vice versa? He knew without a shadow of a doubt they were meant to be a trio. If Kylie left them, he wasn't sure what they would do. She brought out the best in both of them. He had a habit of being headstrong and opinionated, but Kylie softened those rough edges and without her steadying influence, Heath would have succumbed to his workaholic tendencies long ago.

They needed her and not singularly, but as a unit. This weekend had proven to him that there was no way in hell he could go back to a one man, one woman affair. He prided himself on being a red-blooded heterosexual male, but watching Heath and Kylie together had changed some intrinsic part of him and he knew he'd never view sex the same again. He was convinced that where this relationship was concerned, it was all or nothing and he desperately wanted it all.

Giving up on sleep, Colt pulled on some sweatpants and quietly padded to the kitchen. Maybe a midnight snack would cure his sleeplessness. Maybe it was an empty stomach and not his anxious fears keeping him awake. *Yeah right.*

Digging around in the fridge, he found some sandwich fixings. Pulling them out, he started putting the ingredients together without thinking.

"That looks good."

He looked up to find a hungry-looking Heath eyeballing his sandwich.

"Get your own."

Heath grinned at him as Colt pulled his plate closer as if to protect a precious treasure.

"I think you must be the only man on the planet who's
191

irritable after sex."

Colt frowned. "I'm not irritable."

Heath didn't reply, merely lifted his eyebrows in disbelief.

"At least, it's not the sex."

"Hunger?"

"No." He wondered if he should try to explain his worries. He'd already attempted to bring the subject up once and Heath had dismissed it.

Heath sat down across from him and started to assemble a sandwich for himself. "Worrying about Monday isn't going to stop it from coming."

He glanced up, surprised at Heath's astuteness.

"We made a mistake. A fucking whopper of a mistake."

Leaning back against his chair, Heath crossed his arms across his bare chest. "I'd call it a miscalculation, not a mistake."

"Whatever you call it, wiseass, we're in the shithouse now."

Heath's anger seemed to swell at the comment and Colt suddenly realized he wasn't alone in his worry. "Damn it, Colt. Do you know exactly what it is you're considering here?"

"A permanent arrangement." He ran his hands through his hair in frustration. He'd expected Heath to be the easy one to convince. He knew Heath wanted this as much as he did, but if he rejected the idea, there was no way Kylie would accept it.

"Colt, people don't live in ménage situations. It's a fantasy, not a lifestyle."

"Who says? If I've learned anything from Kylie these last few years, it's that I'm not living my life to make other people happy. Besides, we've all lived together so long, nobody even blinks an eye at us anymore."

"There's a difference between platonic roommates and what you're proposing."

"Think about it. Kylie knows what she's getting with us. She's already proven she can handle the day-to-day living together aspect. She's put up with our overbearing, sloppy asses for years."

"There is also a difference between picking up a few dirty dishes and dealing with two Doms in bed. Right now, she can tell us to go to hell if we get over-possessive because we have no real claim on her."

"And if I know Kylie, she'll keep right on telling us where to go, lovers or not."

"Colt, there's no way she'll agree to this. We promised her a fantasy weekend with a return to our 'just friends' status on Monday. How can we go back on our word?"

"All I'm suggesting is that we ask her."

Heath rose and walked toward the kitchen window to gaze into the black night and Colt questioned his friend's feelings. Heath certainly had more to lose if their unusual situation became public knowledge. His friend was next in line for a partnership at the architectural firm where he worked. If the powers that be at his office found out he was an active participant in a ménage a trois, he could be putting his career aspirations at serious risk.

"That is if you're willing, Heath. It's not a small thing I'm proposing here. I'm not saying let's try it and see how it goes. I'm serious about making this a forever thing."

"So you're proposing? To me and Kylie? I'm not sure if I should laugh or punch you in the face."

"I, I mean *we* would be proposing to Kylie. But I guess now that you mention it, we'd be making a commitment to each other too. You're my best friend, Heath. We've been in each

193

other's lives for nearly two decades. I wouldn't know what to do if you weren't in my life anymore. I mean, shit, we root for all the same sports teams. That's rare, man."

Heath laughed at his attempts to lighten the mood. "I do want this, Colt. I'm not blind and I can appreciate how perfect this weekend has been. Neither of us has had much luck in the love department and now I can't help but wonder if it's because we've been in love with Kylie all this time. Maybe we were avoiding the obvious because we thought it might end in a competition for her attentions."

He groaned at Heath's words. "Christ, do you have to mention the 'L' word? You know the thought of that emotion gives me gas."

"Well, you're going to have to overcome that little obstacle because I know for a fact Kylie won't accept any offer we make that doesn't include that sentiment."

Colt ran his hand through his hair once again. "I love her. Shit, I'm crazy about the girl."

Heath walked over and joined him at the kitchen table again. "It really won't bother you when I'm alone with Kylie? There are going to be nights when you're on duty and I'm telling you right now, I won't just be in bed sleeping with her. I'll be fucking her. That doesn't bug you? Even a little?"

Colt shook his head instantly. "Not a bit. I swear to you. Does it bother you that the same holds true when you're out of town?"

Heath gave a humorless laugh. "Not a bit. Geez, what's wrong with us? Don't you think there's something seriously fucked up about that?"

"Not really. I trust you with my life, buddy, and I know you'll take care of Kylie when I'm not around. The three of us fit and I'm not so sure the same would hold true if it was just you and Kylie or just me and Kylie. It's hard to explain but I really feel like this relationship only works as a trio."

Heath nodded. "I feel the same way. I guess when you think about it, we all bring something different to the table. Besides, with our fucked up work hours, it would take both of us to make one full-time husband for her."

"Heath, we've shared everything our whole lives—bedrooms, clothes, cars. It's second nature to us now. Besides, I gotta tell you, the sex—" He stumbled, trying to find the words, but his friend saved him from the task.

"I know," Heath said. "So now we share Kylie?" Heath's question came out as a statement and Colt let it slide without a response. "She'll never go for it."

"You said that about this weekend and she jumped in with both feet. I can't go back, Heath. If she refuses, there'll be no going back to the way things were."

Heath turned and frowned at him. "You'd move out?"

He shrugged. "I'll never be able to be in the same room without wanting her again."

Heath considered his words for a long time. "Neither will I. So I guess we'd better put on our most persuasive faces and convince the girl, since failure doesn't seem to be an option."

He smiled and walked over, placing a friendly hand on Heath's shoulder. "Well, my friend, I've been thinking about that and it seems to me that Kylie responds better to actions than words."

"Are you suggesting we seduce her into agreeing to marry us?"

"Like you said, failure's not an option and the way I see it, all is fair in love and war."

"You're speaking in clichés," Heath muttered.

"Better that than the puns I usually annoy you with."

Chapter Ten

The sun was rising outside the curtains when Kylie opened her eyes to find two large predators staring at her.

"You guys look like a couple of hungry tigers," she teased. She could feel their arousals pushing against her hips and wondered if her body was up to any more playing. She was pleasantly sore in muscles she hadn't known she possessed.

"We were starting to worry you were going to sleep the entire day." Heath reached over and pulled her on top of him. He covered her face with soft kisses and she giggled as his fingers brushed her waist so lightly it tickled.

"It's dawn, you slave driver. Besides, you should have woken me up. I certainly don't want to be accused of wasting our last day on something as silly as sleep." She thought she heard an unhappy growl from Colt, but when she looked over her shoulder his face belied the sound so she dismissed it. "So what's the plan for today?"

"Seems to me there's one fantasy we've yet to indulge in." Colt's deep voice reminded her of his Tequila Truth answer and she shivered with anticipation. Heath must have mistaken her response.

"Easy, Red. Remember your safe word. You can say it anytime."

"I don't want to say it." She pushed up onto her hands and

knees, caging Heath below her while offering Colt a perfect view of what she wanted him to claim.

She was thrilled when Colt's natural dominance came shining through. "Don't move. Stay exactly like that."

She looked over her shoulder as he moved to the bedside table. She watched as he removed two condoms and a tube of lubrication. He saw her gaze on him and he offered her a seductive smile that did little to calm the butterflies now flittering in her stomach. She was about to get her ultimate sexual fantasy. Colt and Heath were going to take her together. She quivered with excitement at the thought.

Colt returned to his spot directly behind her and she struggled to relax when his large hand came to rest on her ass.

Heath reached up and ran his knuckles along her cheek in the way she'd come to love in the few short days they'd been together. The gesture was so typically Heath. His had always been the shoulder she cried on when life got too tough and his touch now was so full of comfort and love it was all she could do not to cry with delight.

She shook slightly when she felt the cold lube land on her ass, but Heath shushed her and continued to stroke her face. She leaned forward, desperate to feel more of him. Her breasts pressed against his hard chest as she offered him her lips, silently begging him to claim her mouth as surely as Colt would claim her ass.

As Heath deepened the kiss with the stroke of his tongue, Colt deepened his own strokes, pushing one, then two thick fingers inside her anus. The plug had worked its magic and she felt her muscles relax against the unfamiliar invasion. Soon he added a third finger and she broke away from the kiss with a pleasured cry.

"More," she demanded without thought. For a moment, she

feared they'd deny her, tease her, but her word seemed to be the impetus they were waiting for. Heath picked up the condom Colt had laid beside him on the bed and put it on, while Colt continued to torment her ass with his fingers. Once Heath was sheathed, his strong grip on her hips pulled her until her wet opening was level with the crown of his cock. She struggled to breathe as he slowly impaled her body on his rigid erection, his tight hold keeping her from thrusting down on him as she desired.

When he was fully seated, he held her completely still. She fought against his hold, desperately trying to fuck his cock until Colt's hand landed on her ass with a loud smack. She froze. The spot he struck stung for only a second until he ran his cool lips across the injured flesh. She fought against the pleasure and pain as he repeated the action on her other buttock.

The feelings his actions evoked in her body were better than in her wildest dreams. This moment was the one. The one she'd spent a lifetime looking for, waiting for, praying for. Heath's hard cock was filling her cunt while Colt marked her ass with a loving spanking. Unable to deny her body's desire, she succumbed to one of the most powerful orgasms she'd ever had.

Colt and Heath must have realized the impact their actions were having on her as Heath wrapped his arms around her while Colt lovingly caressed and kissed the heated skin on her ass.

"More." She repeated her earlier demand as she came back to earth and silently rejoiced when the men—her men—chuckled in surprise.

"Demanding little wench." Heath directed his words over her shoulder at Colt.

"I can see why she's been so mischievous these past few

months. It takes more than one man to satisfy her."

Kylie considered Colt's reply for only a moment, marveling at the truth of his observation, but then her thoughts were washed away by touch of his cock prodding for entrance at her virgin hole.

Together the three of them worked slowly toward heaven. As Colt pushed forward into her tight ass, Heath murmured words of encouragement. Whenever she tried to move, she was halted by not two, but four hands, refusing to allow her to take too much, too quickly. It was clear neither man wanted to rush this for fear of hurting her and Kylie's heart swelled with the thought.

"Almost there," Heath whispered in her ear. "God, Kylie, I can't tell you how good this is. I can feel Colt's cock through the thin wall inside you. It's rubbing against mine. I never knew it could be like this. Thank you, baby. Thank you for giving this to us."

She shivered at his words and Colt shoved in the last few inches, buried deep within her.

"Darlin', are you ready to take a little ride on the roommate roller coaster?"

She grinned over her shoulder. Only Colt could make her want to laugh during the most magical moment of her life.

"Buckle up and keep your cocks inside my body at all times, boys."

"Hold on, Red," Heath said as he gripped her hips and slowly pulled out. When only the head of his cock remained lodged inside, he started back in as Colt retreated. In and out, they moved in unison. She was overwhelmed with sensation, pleasure and pain so intense she wondered if she would survive the sensual assault. Soon their thrusting grew faster, harder and she felt as if she were drowning in desire. She started to come, the orgasm far more intense than any of its predecessors. No sooner had it ended, than another gripped her—and another. She was screaming and shuddering, but her beloved men showed her no remorse. On and on, her body twisted and turned until she thought she surely must be on a roller coaster.

Finally, she felt Colt plummet to earth with her, his climax sending a barrage of words from his mouth. Words like wife and marriage and forever covered her as completely as his body and then they were swept away by Heath's orgasm and his own love words joined Colt's in her subconscious. She savored the words and held them close to her heart. For the first time in years, she allowed herself to dream the impossible dream of holding these two men to her forever. For one glorious moment she imagined a lifetime with Heath, her best friend and confidant, and Colt, her big brother and fiercest protector.

When the last tremor died away in her body, Kylie drifted into sleep, feeling truly loved for the first time in her life.

Chapter Eleven

"Where's Heath?" Kylie asked as Colt came out of the laundry room with a basket full of clothes.

"We were hungry, but there's not much left in the kitchen to eat, so he went out for doughnuts."

"Krispy Kreme?" Her stomach growled at the promise of her favorite sweet treat.

"Is there any other kind?"

"God, I hope they're hot."

Colt laughed. "You know I think my ego's taking a blow here." He walked over to her as if studying her face. "Yep, a bit flushed and if I'm not mistaken, your breathing is uneven. I'm starting to think you could orgasm from the thought of doughnuts and here I was thinking it was only my finesse and skill as a lover that was capable of driving you to that."

"What can I say?" she joked. "I'm a doughnut whore."

She noticed the laundry basket in his hands "What are you doing?"

"Laundry. We're going to be in a whole world of hurt come tomorrow if we don't try and get some of our usual weekend chores outta the way."

She turned up her nose at his words. "I kind of liked forgetting about the real world for awhile."

Colt kissed her softly as his free hand ran through her hair. "Oh baby, we can make the world go away anytime you want to. In fact, I was thinking about you when I was doing the laundry."

"Terrific," she teased. "I've always wanted a pile of smelly socks to remind someone of me."

"It wasn't the socks, darlin', but the dryer."

"Dryer?"

"Come see." He grabbed her hand and tugged her toward the laundry room. As soon as they entered the small room, he set down the basket, then turned and lifted her up on top of the running dryer. The warm vibrations instantly triggered her arousal.

"Oh, wow."

"I knew you'd like that." He seemed pleased by her response. Working the buttons free on the jeans she'd donned only a few minutes earlier, he pulled the zipper down, and gripped her hips. "What are you doing with pants on? I oughtta tan your hide for getting dressed without permission. Let's get these off."

She knew instantly where he was heading. He was tall enough that what he obviously had in mind would work perfectly. She giggled with glee at the thought and quickly divested herself of her pants and panties. The sensation of the dryer against her bare ass increased her arousal.

She and Colt bumped heads in their rush to free him from the confines of his own jeans and they laughed until his cock touched the opening to her wet channel.

"Are you on the pill, darlin'?"

Glancing down, she realized he wasn't wearing a condom.

"Yes," she answered, scooting closer to the edge, pushing

the head of his cock inside of her.

He winced at her action. "I'm clean, but it's up to you. There are condoms in the bedroom."

"Don't you dare leave me. Come inside, Colt. I want to feel you. Just you. Please."

Her invitation issued, he shoved in to the hilt with one hard thrust.

"God, yes. Darlin', you have no idea how good that feels."

"Yes, I do," she confirmed.

No other words were necessary as he began to move in and out of her body. The hot vibrations of the dryer outside and Colt's hard, searing movements inside sent her over the top in an instant. She cried out, but he captured the sound with his mouth. Claiming all her moans with his lips against hers, he continued to rock into her, pushing her higher and higher. When she came again, he fell with her, shouting out his love, pulling her tightly against his body.

As they came back to themselves, Kylie leaned back with a satisfied grin. "All the doughnuts in the world couldn't make me feel like that."

The sound of Colt's cell phone interrupted their shared laughter. He pulled up his jeans and grabbed it off the hallway table right before the voice mail kicked in.

"I'm off duty," he barked into the receiver and she sighed. He was obviously being pulled in to work and she was disappointed at the prospect of her fantasy weekend being cut short.

"Fine, fine. I'll give you one hour, that's it. This is bullshit, Dave, and you know it." Colt clicked the cell shut aggressively and gave her an apologetic look.

She offered him a sympathetic smile. "Don't explain. Just

go. The sooner you get there, the sooner you can get back."

He walked over to her, explanation on his lips, but she halted his words. "I mean it, Colt. It's okay. Just hurry back to me."

He bent forward and placed a chaste kiss on her cheek and she was surprised by the innocence of the gesture. She'd become so in tune to his aggressive, possessive claiming of her lips that the sweetness of his kiss sealed her fate.

"I'll miss you every minute," he said.

"Same here."

"Save me a doughnut?"

"No promises there, big guy."

He laughed and grabbed a clean shirt off the pile of clothes he'd finished washing. "God, I love you," he said and Kylie felt her heart skip a beat at his admission. He didn't seem to expect a reply as he gave her another quick kiss and said goodbye.

She stumbled out of the laundry room in time to watch him cut a swath through the house looking for his keys. She grinned at the familiarity of the scene despite the inner turmoil she felt swirling around her heart.

Damn man could never find his keys and hearing him curse as he continued his search soothed her. Perhaps things were still okay. No doubt he meant his proclamation of love in a casual way. A friend-to-friend way. She loved him and Heath after all and he hadn't said "I'm in love with you". Simply "I love you". Feeling somewhat reassured by her rationalization, she decided to steer clear of the imminent eruption of his temper as she watched him accidentally bump his head on the door of the hall closet.

"I'm going to go grab a shower. Why don't you look in the kitchen for your keys? I seem to recall seeing a set on the counter last night."

Then, coward that she was, she beat a hasty retreat to the safety of her bedroom, anxious to escape not only Colt, but all the feelings he was stirring up inside of her.

Chapter Twelve

"Fuck," Colt yelled, rubbing his chest where Heath's shoulder caught him as they collided at the front door.

"Where's the fire?"

"Sorry. I'm in a hurry. Got called into work. Couldn't find my goddamned keys for ages."

Heath smirked as he dropped the bag of doughnuts on the hall table. "So what else is new? Where's Kylie?"

"She's getting a quick shower."

As Colt spoke, Heath looked at his friend for the first time since entering the house. "You two had sex."

Colt grinned and wiggled his eyebrows. "What can I say? She can't keep her hands off of me. When I get back, we can issue our proposal, but until then, Heath, I fully expect you to do your part to continue convincing her how great a lifetime of fantasy weekends would be."

Heath laughed, rubbing his hands together. "Gee, twist my arm. Kylie, all to myself for the afternoon. Don't feel like you have to rush back on my account."

"Asshole. If my cock weren't so pleasantly sore, I'd probably be pissed, but fact is I'm beat." Colt grabbed his leather jacket. "Take it easy on her. Poor girl's had a busy morning."

He shook his head as Colt left.

Mari Carr

"Cocky bastard," Kylie muttered behind him. "Couldn't wait to brag, could he?"

He turned to see her dressed in her terry cloth robe, her hair wet and dripping. He drank in the sight of her looking so relaxed and at home. She looked the same as she had everyday for the past seven years, yet he was suddenly taken aback by how beautiful she was. It was as if the blinders he'd worn for nearly a decade had fallen away and revealed a living, breathing Venus.

"I missed you," he said softly. He walked over and wrapped his arms loosely around her waist. Even though she'd succumbed to Colt's singular advances, a foolish part of him feared she may reject his.

Her soft lips landed on his cheek, giggling as she wiggled her nose against his unshaven jaw. "I missed you too."

"Kylie."

"Shhh." She placed her fingers against his mouth. "Colt said you went out for doughnuts."

He laughed at her comment. She was a sucker for Krispy Kremes. "Yep and the hot light was on."

She groaned in pleasure as he grabbed her hand and the bag, dragging her to the kitchen. "Come on. We'll eat and then I have an idea."

"Ooh, I like your ideas," she replied. "Give me a hint?"

"It involves you, me, jets, bubbles, and lots and lots of hot water."

She pulled back on his hand, attempting to change his direction. "You know, it seems to me that those doughnuts may be a bit better cold." With a sassy grin, she tugged him toward his bathroom.

Heath followed willingly. Truth be told, he'd eaten two

doughnuts on the way home.

"I can't tell you what this means to me," he joked. "I've honestly never seen anything more important to you than a hot doughnut."

She laughed at his jest, bending down to fill the Jacuzzi tub with water. "Yeah, well, you guys have never offered me a sweeter alternative."

He bent down to kiss her, slowly untying her robe and slipping it off her shoulders. He was pleased to find her completely naked underneath.

"I think you're the sweetest thing in this house, hands down." The heat of their kisses mingled with the steam rising off the water. Both of them were so swept away with their shared touches that they nearly let the water overflow and had to open the drain to release some before they could climb in.

Giggling, she sank down into the tub as he turned on the jets. "Ah, this is heavenly."

He joined her, pulling her onto his lap, facing him. "Now it's heavenly."

They continued to kiss and touch until Heath felt her rise up to take him inside. "Kylie," he said, his hands gripping her hips to halt her movement.

"I'm on the pill," she said answering his unspoken concerns. "Colt and I—"

She stopped and he knew that Colt had taken her without a condom earlier. If he'd been a stronger man, he'd have gotten out of the Jacuzzi to grab the condom, well aware that decisions like this shouldn't be made in the heat of the moment. But the fact was he couldn't have moved away from her if his life had depended on it. He knew they all practiced safe sex and there wasn't anything he wanted more than to be inside her with nothing in between.

"I want you, Kylie," he whispered against her lips and he pulled her down on to his thick erection.

They moved slowly at first, but soon patience gave way to passion as their powerful thrusts stirred up the water and it began to crash in waves around them. They came together and as they drifted back to reality, Heath pulled her head down to rest on his shoulder—desperate to keep her close to him. Fear of the unknown crept into his mind and he worried that this moment alone with her would be the last.

"Hey," she cried and Heath released his crushing grip on her.

"Sorry," he said with a rueful grin.

"Is something wrong?"

Heath started to say the words that were fighting for release, but he couldn't seem to get them out. The risks suddenly felt too great and in the end, he lost the nerve and instead made a joke. "Red, I know you have an aversion to cleaning bathrooms, but I think we're going to have to get a mop in here. There's more water on the floor than in the tub."

She giggled and snuggled closer. "This is nice," she murmured.

"Better than nice," he agreed.

"I keep thinking it should feel strange, but it doesn't."

He considered her comment. After years of "just friends" status, he was also surprised by how natural it felt to hold her in his arms. "We've always been close," he teased, pulling her body flush against his. "Now we're just closer."

"Mmmm," she agreed, dragging her lips across his throat. "I like being closer."

His erection stirred at the first touch of her lips despite the fact he'd had more sex this weekend than in the last year combined.

Kylie felt his cock come back to life. "And closer," she added as she took him back into her body.

"And even closer," he said, slowly thrusting up.

They repeated the mantra, as this joining, unlike the others, was slow and sweet and when it ended, Heath placed a soft kiss on the top of Kylie's head.

"Stay with us—forever," he whispered.

After a nice, long soak in the Jacuzzi with Heath, they parted ways for a little while, each retreating to their own rooms. Heath needed to put the finishing touches on a sketch he was presenting to the partners at work first thing in the morning. Colt was probably pissed as hell by now for being held up at the station so long, but Kylie was grateful to have a few moments of peace and quiet to sort out her thoughts.

Looking at her bed, she wondered how she'd ever be able to survive returning to the lonely, cold thing once the weekend ended. Walking to the mirror that hung above her dresser, she dragged a comb through her tangled auburn hair as she looked at herself for the first time since this fantasy weekend had begun. Her face was flushed, her lips pleasantly swollen from their nonstop kisses. Her curls were disheveled and tousled with a well-bedded look. Leaning forward, she felt as if she were seeing herself for the first time. She looked...damn, she looked beautiful, feminine.

After a weekend listening to Heath and Colt's never-ending compliments, she was seeing herself through different eyes, through their eyes. She'd always considered herself passably pretty, not that she ever tried to improve that state. She was content with her looks and refused to spend hour upon hour attempting to enhance anything. She hated make-up, detested hair salons and clipped her fingernails when they got too long because they annoyed her. She'd never owned a bottle of fingernail polish or a curling iron—although with a head full of spirals, why would she need to? None of that seemed to matter now as she recalled Heath calling her beautiful and Colt whispering the word *gorgeous* in her ear.

Sighing, she chastised herself for her sudden vanity. Damn men. They had her acting like a silly girl. Enough. When the deal ended later tonight, she was going to come back and sleep in that damn empty bed even if it killed her, and when she woke up tomorrow, things would be back to normal. She would be one of the guys again and Colt and Heath would return to simply being her fun-loving, affable friends. Of course that also meant she would have to return to lusting after them in silence. Problem was, now she would know exactly what she was missing rather than merely filling in the blanks with her overactive imagination.

Her thoughts kept drifting back to their professions of love. Clearly, it was the lack of blood to their brains from too much sex that was doing the talking. There was no way they could mean all the wonderful things they were saying. Colt said he loved her. During their bath, Heath had said he wanted her to stay with them forever. She was certain one—or had both of them?—whispered the word *wife* in her ear when they'd made love together this morning.

Her heart ached with the sudden realization that she wanted both of them more than she'd ever wanted anything in her life. Who in the hell did she think she was to consider even for a second that she could possibly be woman enough for just one of them, let alone both of them together. Damn. The problem was, while the sex was great, amazing, fucking off the charts, she'd given her love to them a long time ago for completely different reasons.

Heath was truly her best friend and there was absolutely nothing she didn't tell him. He listened to all of her work stories, consoled her after every stupid break-up, and offered her advice and a swift kick in the ass when he thought she needed it.

Colt was more like an older brother to her than her own sibling. He protected her, looked out for her best interests and made her feel safe and cherished. In addition to that, he made her laugh—all the time, and in her book that was more important than flowery words or sappy sentiments.

She felt like she was losing the struggle to retrieve what was left of her scattered wits. How long would it be until they realized what they'd offered during the heat of the moment? Were they even now regretting the impulsiveness of their words? How could they know how much their sweet nothings affected her and tapped into her most desperate desires for them? How long would she have to defend her heart and soul against the memories of this glorious weekend and how long would it be before she'd have to be committed to the psychiatric hospital?

Yes, she decided, pushing away from the mirror, a good night's sleep would restore things back to normal. She'd find a way to return to her old self and somehow, someway she'd manage to put away her unruly desires and pull out Kylie the buddy once again. At least she hoped that proved so because the very sad, very true fact was she had fallen madly, deeply, passionately in love with Heath and Colt and she didn't know if she could survive the fallout of a return to their previous lives.

Chapter Thirteen

Colt watched the sun set on their fantasy weekend as Kylie slept in his arms. He'd returned home a couple of hours earlier to find Heath and Kylie cuddled up together on the couch. From the flushed, satisfied look on their faces, he knew they'd done far more than merely relax in front of the action-adventure flick they were watching on television. He'd joined them and now he was trying to determine how he'd ever look at their couch again without thinking of the love games they'd played upon it. The image of Kylie on top of him and riding his cock as she bent forward to suck on Heath's erection had forever changed the way he'd see that piece of furniture.

They'd stumbled back to his bed and fallen asleep instantly. Unfortunately, his restless mind wouldn't let his body continue to slumber and he wasn't alone in his anxiety.

Heath had gotten up a few minutes earlier and he could hear him pacing around the room. The incredible sensations of their earlier lovemaking were still resonating in his body and Colt wished he could wake her up and disappear in her sweetness once again.

Looking toward the end of the bed, he could see Heath had given up his uneasy wanderings and was sitting in a chair that was usually covered with clothing.

"Now what?" Heath whispered and Colt fought against the

pain lodged in his chest. They'd thought they could coerce her with sex, giving her everything they had to give. They'd said the words written in their hearts as they made love to her, but she'd no doubt dismissed it as mindless love talk.

They needed to broach the subject now before she returned to her own room, thinking with the end of the weekend that things were going back to normal. He feared she was content with the thought of getting up in the morning, going to work and then coming home to watch a hockey game with them as if the weekend had never happened. That same scenario made his blood run cold. He'd never get the image of her accepting him and Heath into her body time and time again out of his mind. He was head-over-heels, hopelessly in love with the woman and if she seriously thought they were going to give up without a fight, then she had another think coming. There would be no return to normal.

He grimaced. Normal. What the fuck was that? Living as platonic roommates, the way they had the last seven years, suddenly seemed completely abnormal. How had they existed like that for so long?

"We need dinner." Heath rose and started out of the room. "Wake her up. It's time we had a talk and it obviously won't happen in the bedroom."

He watched Heath stiffen his spine and walk toward the kitchen. He had to hand it to his best friend; he had more courage than he did. The idea of proposing to Kylie had his heart racing and his hands shaking.

Sighing heavily, he bent over her sleeping form and pressed a light kiss to her forehead.

"Wake up, darlin'."

She tried to shrug him off and he grinned at her grumpy expression. She never did like being woken up and to say she wasn't a morning person was an understatement. Granted, this wasn't morning, but given the way they'd gotten their days and nights so screwed up, she probably thought it was.

"Rise and shine."

"I don't want to," she grumbled, rolling over and pulling the covers over her head.

"Heath is making us dinner."

"I'm not hungry."

"You must be. All we ate today were cold doughnuts. Come on, sweetness. It's Sunday night and we're all going back to work in the morning. We need to have a talk." He forced a lightness he didn't feel into his words, but she must have sensed his stress.

She turned over and looked at him closely. "We don't have to have a talk, Colt. I remember the rules. Honestly, you and Heath don't have to worry about me going all girly on you."

He wanted to shake her. Problem was she wouldn't go *all girly* on them. She struck a deal and she'd stand by it regardless of what it may cost all of them.

"Actually, Kylie, that's not what's worrying me. Get up. We really need to have this talk...with Heath."

Colt watched a flurry of emotions cross her face and was overwhelmed by the desire to lay her back down on the bed and kiss her until the world and his worries disappeared.

Instead, he got up, got dressed and headed for the kitchen without another word. He wasn't surprised to find her right behind him. Their tough little darlin' never shied away from the hard conversations. She'd stood up to both of them more times than he could count when she felt like they were making stupid mistakes. Regardless of what she thought this conversation would entail—and he suspected she didn't have a clue about the true purpose of it—she wasn't running and hiding.

Heath was standing at the stove flipping grilled ham and cheese sandwiches and she passed Colt in the doorway.

"Ooh, my favorite. This is going to be a serious talk, isn't it?" Although she was joking, he could read the concern in her eyes.

Heath narrowed his eyes at him.

He answered the unspoken question. "I didn't say anything."

"That's right," Kylie interrupted. "He woke me up from a sound sleep and demanded this discussion. I tried to assure him it wasn't necessary."

"What's not necessary, Red?" Heath seemed confused by her nonchalance and he knew his friend wouldn't like her easy dismissal of the end of their deal anymore than he had. Of course, in all fairness, she didn't seem to realize their feelings had changed and the damned chit was so closed-mouthed about her own emotions he had no clue what she felt.

"I'm not going to get all weepy and start making a bunch of demands. Our deal was for one weekend. Now the weekend's over and we can go back to business as usual. You guys should know me well enough to know I'd never renege on a deal."

"I don't think that's our concern." Heath took the sandwiches off the burner and put them onto plates. "Grab one and let's sit down."

As soon as they were all settled at the table, she leaned back and placed her arms across her chest impatiently. The movement hiked her breasts up and Colt had to swallow hard against the erection she seemed to inspire without effort.

"About the deal," he began. He looked at Heath wondering how in the hell two men were supposed to propose marriage to one headstrong woman at the same time.

"What about it?" she asked. "What the hell is wrong with you guys? You're starting to worry me here. You never freeze up like this. If you have something to say, spit it out so we can all eat. I'm starving."

He grinned at her annoyance and realized regardless of the outcome of this conversation, he didn't intend to give up—ever. Glancing at Heath, he saw the same emotions reflected in his face. Kylie was their girl and if they had to spend a lifetime convincing her of that fact, then so be it.

"Fine, the deal's off." He answered calmly, picking up his sandwich and taking a bite.

"I know that, Baretta. Geez. Is that all you wanted to say?"

"Yep." He continued digging into his sandwich and sensed Heath giving him the evil eye.

"I don't think you understand what Colt's saying, Red."

She looked at Heath waiting for him to explain.

"When he says the deal is off, he means the time-limit part."

"Time's up. I know."

"Dammit, Colt, would you stop stuffing your face and hop in here?"

He grinned at Heath's discomfort. "Way I see it, Heath, Kylie's right. There's nothing to discuss. We've been roommates for years and I don't see that ending in the foreseeable future."

He turned to face her. "We love you, darlin', and we plan to extend this weekend of fantasies to a lifetime engagement. No, scratch that engagement bit, a lifetime marriage."

"Marriage?" Kylie's face was so cute in her confusion he couldn't resist the urge to lean across the table and kiss her wrinkled-up nose.

"Marriage. You, me and Heath. Forever and ever, amen."

Heath groaned at his nonchalant attitude. "Well, that's certainly the worst proposal I've ever heard. I'm embarrassed my name was even linked to it."

"You're proposing?" Her face was still a mixture of utter shock and complete bewilderment.

"Yep. And darlin', I want you to think long and hard before you answer. I can see those wheels in your brain churning and I'm pretty sure you're thinking about laying into us. Telling us we're crazy and that it will never work and a whole bunch of other nonsense. Trust me, we've thought about all that and there's nothing you can say that will change the fact that you're our girl and we aim to keep you with us forever."

Her mouth remained tightly closed as she studied his impassive face. She must have read his determination as she turned to Heath, no doubt expecting him to offer her some semblance of sanity.

"Heath," she started, but Heath cut her off.

"He's right, Kylie. We belong together. We've been fools not to see it long before this. I think if you look deep inside, you'll see it's true. Hell, Red, we've learned to do the hard part. Living together, dealing with each other's quirks. Colt and I know better than to try and discuss anything serious with you before you've had your first cup of coffee. You and I know not to say a damn word to Colt the day after the Toronto Maple Leafs lose a game. You and Colt respect my privacy when I'm buried in drawing plans for a new project."

"Think about it, darlin'. We've already divvied up all the jobs. You do the shopping, I take care of the yard, Heath fixes all the things that break. We share the cooking and cleaning chores. Everything newlyweds fight about after the honeymoon won't exist for us."

"Colt, you're a cop. I'm fairly certain you realize what you are proposing is illegal. As in bigamy."

He laughed. "You don't legally marry us both. Just one of us. Then the three of us make our own private vows."

"Fine," she leaned back and gave him a smug look as if expecting her next question to jar some sense into them. "Who am I going to legally marry?"

He grinned at her transparency. Obviously, she thought this was going to be a sticking point. "We'll arm wrestle to decide that."

Heath laughed at the suggestion. "Good call. I was wondering about that myself."

"Actually," he crooked his thumb at Heath. "You'll marry Heath. He's got the job which requires a bit of propriety. You'll be the future architect partner's wife."

"Colt," Heath frowned at his answer, but he was convinced by the practicality of it.

"I'm a cop, Heath. Given the bizarre nature of most of the criminals we have to deal with, none of my friends there will care about something as innocuous as me living with a married couple. You're climbing up the ladder of success and I think the partners at that firm of yours will feel better about you if you are respectably married. Besides, you've got better health insurance."

Heath grinned. "Well, you've got a good point there. Your health plan sucks."

Kylie frowned. "This isn't a joke. Can't you two try for once to be serious?"

Colt shrugged off her comment. "I've never been more serious about anything in my life. We love you. You can fight us 'til the cows come home, but we don't intend to back down from this until you have our ring on your finger."

Chapter Fourteen

"That's it!" Kylie stood up so quickly her chair fell over. "You two have lost your minds and I'm not discussing this any further. You were right about one thing tonight. The deal is off. I'm going to bed. My bed—alone."

Colt stopped her before she could take two steps. "I understand, darlin'. You need to think our proposal over. Take your time. We're not going anywhere. And just so you know, you aren't either."

"What's that supposed to mean?"

"It means we expect you to deal with this problem like you have everything else in your life. Head on. Don't even think about trying to run away from this or us because we'll drag you back. We'll give you time to think about what we're asking, but we're not going to stop trying to convince you and you are not going back to your bed...ever."

As if to accentuate his point, Colt gave her a passionate kiss that proved the truth behind his words. While her mind continued to rebel against their unconventional offer, her body had already commended itself into their oh-so-capable hands. She wasn't even sure when Colt's kiss ended and Heath's began, but by the time they stepped away from her, she had to fight against surrendering to their wishes then and there.

Colt gave her a tired grin and she realized that perhaps she wasn't alone in her anxiety. Was he feeling the same stress and fear about this situation? He always seemed so in control and calm, but perhaps his heart truly was engaged and she was hurting him with her refusal.

And what about Heath? Was he truly okay with the idea of the three of them sharing a lifetime together? While she and Colt tended to snub their noses at society as a whole, Heath was the one constantly striving for respect and success. What if the truth of their arrangement came out? While it would make things uncomfortable for her and Colt, it could destroy Heath.

"I'm going to my room." She stumbled back, hoping they would grant her escape, but Colt stopped her with a firm grip on her upper arm.

"No, darlin'. We warned you. You can deny the words, but you can't deny the feelings. We won't let you." As Colt spoke, he pulled her toward him and she felt a bit like a fly caught in a spider's web. As his arms wrapped around her waist, she felt Heath step in close behind her. They trapped her so quickly and efficiently she hadn't had time to react.

"You're our girl, Kylie," Heath whispered against the nape of her neck as he rubbed his lips gently across the sensitive flesh there.

Again with the word *our*. Always the distinction. Couldn't they understand the preposterousness of what they were suggesting? She closed her eyes against the sensations they were evoking with their soft touches and warm kisses.

Hell, who was she fooling? She'd been praying for this moment since her freshman year of college. Now it was here and she was fighting against it. Maybe her two lovers really had pushed her into insanity. While common sense told her she was crazy to accept the idea of living together in matrimony with two men, her heart and body agreed she would be a fool to refuse.

She did belong with them. She was their girl and they were her men.

Throwing caution to the wind, she gave in to her heart's desire. Turning her head, she reached up, desperate to stake her own claim on Heath's mouth. She wanted their kisses, their hands, hell, she wanted them so badly she felt cross-eyed with the cravings wracking her body.

Rather than gloat at her unquestionable longing for them, as she had feared they would, she felt the tension give way in the air surrounding them and she heard Colt sigh in undeniable relief.

"I love you," Heath whispered against her lips and she felt the same emotion swamping her. Did she dare give them the same words back?

Colt never gave her a chance to reply. He turned her toward him and looked at her with his typical charming grin. "Little darlin', I love you too. Take pity on us, Kylie. We're stupid, ignorant men and I have a strong suspicion you're the only one who can cure us of that affliction."

She laughed as Heath's voice drifted over her shoulder. "Speak for yourself on the stupid part, Colt. What do you say, Red? Put us out of our misery?"

"I say I love both of you crazy fools. But I'm going to tell you right now, I refuse to miss one more dinner because of the insatiable sex drives of my roommates. I'm starving."

Heath laughed. "Guess we had better hurry up and get some food into you. I know how irritable you get on an empty stomach. It's not a pretty sight, Red."

"Sweet talking fool. Come on. I need more than that damn cold sandwich. I'll throw a frozen lasagna in the oven, but if you're really serious about us following through with this lifetime living arrangement, one of us is going to have to learn to cook."

After dinner, Colt rose from the table and carried her back to his bedroom as Heath followed. She was amazed by the gentleness of their touch. It seemed with her profession of love, a change had taken place in both men. Rather than the passionate, desperate lovemaking she'd grown accustomed to, calmness had descended over their shared bed. Heath and Colt caressed and kissed her as if they had the rest of their lives to explore every part of her, learn all of her secrets, and she relished each touch and stroke.

In turn, she took the time to learn their bodies, committing to memory what they liked, what made their hearts race and their breathing accelerate. She realized Heath's ears were definitely an erogenous zone and by simply teasing his earlobe with her teeth and tongue, she could drive him to the point of wildness. Colt's needs were much more basic and seemed so true to form. He loved a rough touch and she felt as if she could quite literally drive him to his knees by nipping sharply at his nipples or pulling her fist tightly against his firm cock.

Both men loved to have their balls fondled and she delighted in teasing them with that knowledge. Unfortunately, her torments were usually met with equal torture from her lovers. They loved driving her to the edge of her climax, only to pull away. Colt informed her she needed a lesson in patience and it was only Heath's hands encasing her wrists that stopped her from cuffing the arrogant man on the ears.

"Please," she gasped after Heath's fingers left her weeping cunt once again. She was on the verge of the mother of all orgasms and they'd denied her release five times. "Please, no more. I can't take it."

Colt kissed her gently as she felt his cock push into her pussy a mere inch. "You can take everything we give you and more, darlin'. That's why we love you so much. You were made for us."

With his words, he pushed in completely, holding still as he reached the hilt, so he could take the time to give her a deep, hard kiss. When he released her lips, she thrust her hips up.

"Make love to me, Colt. God, please just love me."

He responded to her request in true Colt fashion, taking her hard and deep and in the way she loved. Over and over he pounded his cock into her body as his loving words drove into her heart and her soul. They came together long and loud and she had only begun to drift down to earth, when she felt Heath enter her. His lovemaking was just as desperate, just as passionate and before she knew what hit her, she was coming again, bright lights flashing behind her eyes and a full orchestra playing in her ears. "I love you," she screamed, clutching Heath.

As his climax died, he lowered himself onto her, keeping the majority of his weight on his arms. "I love you too, Red. I love you so much it's killing me."

She smiled, drowsy and well-loved and feeling completely at peace for the first time in her life.

Epilogue

It was the middle of the night when she skittered to the top of the bed, away from his groping hands. It seemed none of them were able to pull away from each other for more than a couple of hours.

"Colt." Her voice issued a warning both men chose to ignore.

"Come on, Red. We haven't finished celebrating." Heath tried to grasp her ankle, but she deftly dodged him, taking him by surprise with her quick evasion.

"And what exactly do you think we're celebrating?" she asked.

"Our upcoming nuptials."

"Funny," she replied. "I don't remember saying yes to any proposal."

Heath rose, ready to spring, but she anticipated his move and dove over him onto the floor by the bed.

"Is this a chase?" Colt sat up and grinned evilly, his lower body proving his readiness to play, tenting the sheet around his waist.

"No," she answered, obviously anxious to put that thought to rest quickly. "Actually, I have something else in mind."

He frowned. "Other than sex?"

Kylie rolled her eyes. "Yes, Mr. One-Track-Mind. Other than sex. You two wait here and I'll call you when I'm ready."

He scowled, ready to protest, but Heath halted his words. "Okay. Just so long as sex figures somewhere into the game, Red."

"Geez, you two certainly are a matched-set. Giant vessels, horny creatures, filled with nothing but testosterone." She accompanied her words with a funny imitation, placing two fingers against the side of her head like devil's horns and giving them her best evil eye.

Colt laughed at her silly face. "I'll only play your game so long as you promise not to put any clothes on. I have to say I sure do like the sight of you right now. All pissed off and naked."

"Fine, promise you won't come out until I call."

"Promise," Heath agreed. "But make it quick. I'm with Colt, you look damned irresistible."

Colt leaned back against the headboard with his arms crossed against his chest as she left the room. "What did she mean when she said she didn't accept our proposal? Didn't what happened here tonight seem like a yes?"

"She said she loved us, not that she agreed to marry us. Damn, she got us with semantics."

"She *didn't* say anything about marriage. Hell, what do you think that means? I'm not going to do this living together thing forever, Heath. I want that girl to commit to us. I need that commitment. She's ours."

"I agree." Heath stood up and grabbed a pair of jeans off the floor. "What the hell's taking her so long?"

Colt rose and pulled on his pants as well. "I don't know, but I don't aim to wait too much longer. Shit, for all we know, she's duped us both and is sneaking out the back door as we speak."

He meant his words as a joke, but both of them exchanged alarmed glances.

"She wouldn't." They took off down the hallway, stumbling to a halt in the living room. Kylie had drawn the curtains and was pouring out shots of tequila.

She scowled at them when the entered the room. "I didn't call you yet."

"What are you doing?" Heath gestured to the drinks.

"I think we need a quick game of Tequila Truth."

"What the hell for?" Colt demanded.

"There's a question I need answered and only complete honesty will do." She handed each of them a shot glass before picking up her own.

"Fire away." Heath lifted his glass in a silent toast.

"It's a two-parter actually." She raised her glass to her lips and Colt noticed that her hand trembled slightly. "First, will you both marry me? And secondly, do you swear to love me forever?"

Heath downed his shot in an instant and Colt followed suit.

"Yes and yes," Heath answered.

"Ditto," Colt replied. "Now can we have sex?"

Kylie rolled her eyes and giggled. "Crap. So much for heartfelt confessions and deep introspection. You two really are cavemen. But at least you're my cavemen and I wouldn't have you any other way. Come on. Let's go back to bed."

About the Author

To learn more about Mari Carr, please visit www.maricarr.com. Send an email to Mari at carmichm1@yahoo.com or join her Yahoo! group to join in the fun with other readers as well as Mari at http://groups.yahoo.com/group/maricarr/.

hot stuff

Discover Samhain!

THE HOTTEST NEW PUBLISHER ON THE PLANET

Romance, fantasy, mystery, thriller, mainstream and more—Samhain has more selection, hotter authors, and everything's available in both ebook and print.

Pick your favorite, sit back, and enjoy the ride! Hot stuff indeed.

SAMhain publishing LTD

WWW.SAMHAINPUBLISHING.COM

GREAT
CHEAP
FUN

Discover eBooks!

THE FASTEST WAY TO GET THE HOTTEST NAMES

Get your favorite authors on your favorite reader, long before they're
out in print! Ebooks from Samhain go wherever you go, and work with
whatever you carry—Palm, PDF, Mobi, and more.

Samhain
Publishing
Ltd

WWW.SAMHAINPUBLISHING.COM

LaVergne, TN USA
09 September 2010
196460LV00002B/34/P